HOLDING

TRIPPING - BOOK 3

ARIEL BISHOP

 Created with Vellum

For the OMGCP Discord. You know what you did ;)

CONTINENTAL HOCKEY LEAGUE

New England Division

Baltimore Basilisks
Providence Griffins
Boston Banshees
New York Gargoyles
New Jersey Reapers
Toronto Trolls
Ottawa Sirens
Montreal Manticores

Seaboard Division

Carolina Chimeras

Miami Hellhounds
Pensacola Hydras
Philadelphia Phantoms
Washington Wyverns
Atlanta Krakens
Nashville Nagas
Kansas City Centaurs

Heartland Division

Wisconsin Wendigos
Texas Thunderbirds
Chicago Wizards
New Mexico Jackalopes
Detroit Sphinxes
Colorado Yetis
Alberta Abominables
Montana Werewolves

Gold Coast Division

Seattle Selkies
Vegas Vampires
Portland Sasquatches
Arizona Phoenixes
Los Angeles Chupacabras
San Jose Dragons
Idaho Giants
Vancouver Leviathans

ALBERTA ABOMINABLES LINEUP

Forwards

First Line
Karp "Trout" Bazarov - Left
Ivan "Pigeon" Cordova - Center
Logan "Stewie" Stewart - Right (C)
Second Line
Daniel "Suzie" Suzumura - Left (A)
Ben "Hendy" Henderson - Center
Alain "Bucky" Frappier - Right
Third Line
Hanno "Peso" Pesonen - Left
Obioma "Obi-Wan" Chiagoziem - Center
Eric "Rico" Thuyen - Right
Fourth Line
Brijesh "Harry" Chaudhari - Left

Mitchell "Ricky" Richardson - Center
Garrett "Tommy" Thomas - Right

Fifth Line
David "Gonzo" Gonzalez - Left
Christopher "Nova" Mironov - Center
Viktor "Rover" Potrovsky - Right

Defense

First Pair
Francisco "Sunshine" Reyes (A)
Trevor "Angel" Rangel

Second Pair
Will "Swifty" Taylor
Marcus "Z-man" Zhao

Third Pair
Paul "Guns" Gunnarsson
Dipak "Orange" Nirang

Fourth Pair
Kevin "Mikey" Rodriguez Michaelson
Anatoly "Tolly" Petrov

Goalies
Valentin "Tiger" Rajala
Chris "CC" Cooper
Oskar "Lindy" Lindholm

Utility
Henri "Hurry" Hurme (D)

Christopher "Nova" Mironov (F)
Jouto "Sake" Osaka (F)
Pierre-Marc "Lambie" Lambert (F)
Brad "Chad" Larsen (F)
Seth "Lightning" Carson (D)

1

TOLYA

Michaelson and Petrov Bond On and Off the Ice

Kevin Michaelson and Anatoly Petrov aren't your usual CHL rookies. At 21, with three seasons of NCAA hockey under his belt, Michaelson is understandably more mature than the average 18-year-old prospect fresh out of the draft. And while Petrov was one of those 18-year-olds, being Vladislav Petrov's son didn't keep him from doing his time in the minors.

"It's a little different," Michaelson agrees when asked about it. "I mean, it's exciting, for sure. But this isn't my first time living on my own like it is for a lot of the guys. I'm glad Tolly's here, otherwise it would be a little weird, just me and the other rookies. I'd feel a little creepy, to be honest."

Petrov nods. "Mikey's a good roommate."

It's clear after spending even a few minutes with them that their friendship is not just a product of the Abs' PR team. Both of them are very comfortable with each other, laughing several times at inside jokes that they can't really seem to explain beyond "you had to be there."

But as much as the fans love their friendship, their on-ice chemistry is what has people excited to see what happens this season. Both Petrov and Michaelson are quick to say that it's a team effort, of course, but there's no denying that they're putting up some impressive point totals for d-men their rookie season, particularly Michaelson, with a goal and an assist in his first regular season game.

"There's still a lot of season left," he says, ducking his head bashfully. "We're just trying to take it one game at a time."

"**O**kay," Stewie says, looking around the locker room, his captain face firmly in place. "You know what to do. Let's go out there and get it done."

Tolya adds his voice to the wordless roar of assent, stands with the rest of the team to file out of the locker room. The familiar ball of nerves and anticipation is tight in his stomach, even months into the season. He suspects it won't ever completely go away, isn't entirely sure he wants it to. He'll have to ask his father the next time he goes home.

But right now, with Mikey a comforting presence behind him, accepting a fist bump from his captain as he files down the tunnel and joins most of the team on the bench, everything is good. The Wendigos are having a pretty good season, but so are the Abs. Tolya can practically taste the anticipation in the air, feel it in the way Mikey's shoulder bumps into his as they lean forward to watch the face-off.

It's a good game, the kind of game Tolya loves to watch. Not too chippy, lots of skill on the ice. The Wendigos are faster than he remembers from last season, and they score in the first, their goalie somehow managing to stop all the Abs' shots on goal. Still, it's just the first period. Even when it ends without them getting an answering goal, the mood is good as they head back to the locker room.

"Man, MacAllister's on fire tonight," Mikey mutters, rubbing a towel over his hair. It stands up in dark clumps that make Tolya's fingers itch to smooth them back down. "Nobody's getting shit past him."

"We've got two more periods," he says instead, swigging from his bottle. "Just gotta keep it together."

Mikey rolls his eyes. "Thanks, Coach."

Tolya shrugs. "You know it's true."

"Yeah," Mikey sighs. "I know."

"Cheer up," Tolya says, bumping their knees together. "I'm buying tonight."

Mikey grins crookedly. "Well, then. Let's light it up."

As the minutes tick down on the second period, Tolya can feel the mood shift, the certainty of defeat creeping in even though no one says anything. When Hartsburg scores again, it's like a shockwave going through the Abs.

With only a couple of minutes left to go, Coach Daniels waves their line over the boards. Tolya shoves his mouthguard back between his teeth and obeys, Mikey at his side like they share the same brain. He does his best to wipe everything from his head, to just get to the puck. The Wendigos are tired, too—if he's going to have a chance, this is as good a time as any.

He's so focused on the puck that he almost doesn't see it begin. The sudden motion of Plats falling in the corner of his eye catches his attention, and his head whips around just in time to see the Wendigo d-men barely avoid him, almost colliding as they deke around to keep their skates away from his fallen body.

But there's no way for Mikey to avoid him. Tolya watches in horror as Mikey tries to jump, his skates catching on a rough spot in the ice. As Mikey goes flying through the air. As Mikey hits the ice with an audible crack, his whole body going limp, his arm bent at a terrible, unnatural angle that turns Tolya's stomach.

He doesn't even realize he's moving until it's already happened. He's too late, he knows he's too late, but he can't stop himself, sliding the last few meters on his knees so he doesn't collide with Mikey's still, broken body. It's wrong, so wrong, for Mikey to be so still. Mikey's never still, even in his sleep, some part of him always moving. But he's still now, and Tolya can feel the dread rising up in his throat like vomit.

"You've got to let us through, son," someone says, kindly but firmly, from behind him.

Tolya turns his head to see the medics. That's good. He shifts back enough to let them work, struggles to his feet. When the woman checking Mikey's pulse nods to her colleague, it feels like the first time he's breathed in hours.

But that relief is short-lived. He keeps waiting, waiting for Mikey to open his eyes, to smile and crack a joke. To be okay, like he was just a minute ago. But the medics slide a board under him, lift him carefully onto the stretcher. Tolya has to bite back a protest when they strap him down; Mikey would hate that.

Then they're wheeling him off the ice, the arena silent as they watch. Tolya takes a breath, then another, tries to get himself back mentally to where he should be. It's the game. He knows this, down to his bones. He has to be ready, to play. No matter what.

It's a shameful relief when the officials call the period,

when he can stop pretending, can file back down the tunnel and into the locker room.

That intermission, with Mikey's stall empty beside him, is the longest one of Tolya's life.

THE MOST DISTRACTED third period Tolya's ever played drags on forever, it seems. He does his best to focus, to just think about playing the game. But it feels wrong, being on the ice without Mikey there, or sitting on the bench waiting for him. The seconds slip by slowly, one after another, like water drops falling from a leaking faucet, each one winding his nerves tighter and tighter.

Finally, after an endless forever, the final buzzer sounds. Tolya is vaguely aware that he should care that they got shut out, that the Wendigos beat them by two, but he just can't right now. He's the first off the bench, first down the tunnel to the locker room, stripping his gear off as fast as he physically can.

Part of him is waiting to be pulled in for press, to have to relive the moment where Mikey hit the ice and try to say something coherent about it, with the lights and the cameras and the microphones in his face. It's part of the job; he knows this, has known it ever since the first time he saw his father being interviewed. But right now it's just another restraint, another thing keeping him from seeing Mikey with his own eyes.

Stewie files in after the rest of the team, nodding

approvingly at where Tolya's down to his compression shorts and his jock. "Good. Get showered and dressed and we'll head to the Royal Alex."

Even though he didn't think it was possible, Tolya finishes getting naked even faster, tripping over his feet on his way into the the showers. He doesn't linger under the water, just stays long enough to scrub the sweat off his skin and hair before grabbing a towel and drying off hastily as he walks back to the room. His clothes stick to his still-damp skin as he drags them on, shoving his feet into socks and shoes, dragging his hands through his hair because he can't stand to go looking for a comb right now.

Through some captainly magic, Stewie appears next to him, fully dressed. "Ready?"

"No press?" Tolya asks, unable to stop himself.

Stewie shakes his head, guiding Tolya out of the room with a hand on his shoulder. "Not tonight, kiddo. Plenty of time for that tomorrow."

Tolya nods and lets himself be steered toward Stewie's pickup. They ride to the hospital in silence, the only sound the low murmur of voices and music from the radio.

The knots in his stomach twist tighter as they come to a stop in the hospital parkade. As much as he wants to see Mikey, as it feels wrong not to be at his side, a part of him doesn't want to leave the truck. If he just stays here—If he doesn't leave—then there's a chance that Mikey's okay, smiling and laughing and charming the nurses even though they're frustrated because he won't stay in bed.

"Come on," Stewie says gently, shoving his door open. "Fortify, rookie."

Tolya takes a deep breath and reaches for his seatbelt.

Thank fuck Stewie's there. Tolya doesn't have to talk to anyone; he can just follow along in his captain's wake, to the desk where the attendant checks her computer and gives them a room number, after confirming that Stewie is on the list of people with access to Mikey's information. To the bank of elevators leading up to the patient rooms, waiting in tense silence as it climbs up to the seventh floor. To one of the several identical doors on the hallway.

Through the door.

It looks unnatural for Mikey to be so still, he thinks again, sick to his stomach when he remembers that moment on the ice, the splash of blood against the white. The only reassurance he has is the steady beep of the machine tracking Mikey's pulse, the slow movement of Mikey's chest.

"I'm going to see if I can find a nurse, get an update," Stewie says, his voice hushed like people always are in hospital rooms. "You want to come with?"

"Nah," Tolya manages, swallowing hard. "I'll stay here."

Stewie squeezes his shoulder once and then he's gone, the door closing behind him with a soft click. Leaving Tolya alone with Mikey's unconscious form, still and silent in the hospital bed. His skin looks pale and washed out against the white sheets and the hospital gown.

Tolya's knees give out under him and he sinks into the

chair, keeping his eyes on Mikey's face, straining his ears for the slow, consistent beeps, doing his best not to count the number of times Mikey's chest rises and falls under the sheet. His arm is casted, resting on top of his stomach, a stark white bandage wrapped around his head.

His phone vibrates in his pocket, startling him out of trying to catalog Mikey's injuries. When he pulls it out, he sees two missed calls from his parents. As he watches, a text from his mom pops up on the lock screen. *Call when you can*

It feels weird and wrong to respond, but hell, it's not like Mikey is awake to complain. Not like he'd complain even if he was—he'd just insist on getting his turn to talk with Tolya's mom. So he unlocks the phone and texts back. *At the hospital. I'll call when I get home.*

She responds almost instantly. *Okay. Love you.*

Love you, too

He's about to lock the phone back when another text pops up, this time from Mikey's sister Andrea. *u at the hospital w kevin?*

It always takes him a minute to remember that Mikey's family calls him by his given name, even more tonight with his brain slow and distracted, adrenaline crash slowly draining his energy. *yeah,* he responds. *room 742. u coming?*

The whole clan is on the road, she confirms. *brace urself.*

He looks at the clock on his phone and does some calculations, trying to figure out when the team would've notified Mr. and Mrs. Michaelson, subtracting that from the three hours between Calgary and Edmonton. *see u soon*, he sends, settling back in the chair. Somehow it feels less heavy, knowing that Mikey's family will be here soon.

Leaning his head against the wall, he waits.

First regular season game

Tolya picks his head up out of his hands when he hears footsteps approaching, doing his best to look like—well, not like someone having a panic attack. That'll look great to the rest of the team, totally like someone who should stay up for the season.

But it's not Stewie or either of the A's who comes around the corner. It's Mikey, which is almost worse. What's he going to think, seeing that his d-partner can't hold it together? What if—

"Hey," Mikey says. "Can I sit down?"

Tolya takes a minute to make sure his voice is gonna be steady when he speaks. "Yeah, sure. What's up?"

"Just looking for a quiet corner," Mikey says, sinking down to sit on the concrete floor next to him, their shoulders bumping together, close enough that Tolya can feel his body heat. "It's a lot, you know?"

"Yeah," Tolya laughs. It's either laugh or cry, and better the first than the second. "Yeah, it is."

They sit in silence for a minute. Tolya's stomach still feels jittery, roiling with the anxiety and the what-ifs, but having

Mikey there, warm and solid next to him, is infinitely better than being here alone. Slowly, he feels his breathing slow down, even out.

"So, like, not to be sappy and shit," Mikey says, startling Tolya a little when his voice breaks the quiet, "but dude, you're the best d-partner I've ever had. I can't imagine playing this game without you."

"Same here," Tolya says without hesitating.

Mikey pushes to his feet and offers a hand. "Cool."

Taking his hand, Tolya unfolds himself, stretching a little to ease muscles gone tight and tense. "Cool," he echoes, because he's feeling better enough to be a shit, and because he knows it will make Mikey roll his eyes.

Sure enough, Mikey doesn't disappoint. "Come on," he says, turning in the direction of the locker room and pulling Tolya along behind him. "Let's light it up."

2

MIKEY

The first thing Mikey notices when he wakes up is the smell. Hospital smell is unmistakable, especially when paired with the soft beeping of monitors.

The pain is the next thing, filtering into his consciousness until it's all he can think about. His head, his right arm, his left hand with the peculiar internal soreness that indicates an IV. Shit. What the fuck happened?

The last thing he remembers is heading out for the second period, but trying to push through the foggy feeling, to dig deeper, just makes his head throb harder, faster. His eyelids feel like they weigh a couple of hundred pounds each, and it seems to take forever before he can open them just a crack.

Light stabs in through that opening and he has instant

regrets, closing them again as fast as he can. It's not fast enough, though. The pain in his head increases to a blinding level, wiping out all other thought for way too long.

"Mikey?" It's a whisper, but he'd recognize Tolly's voice anywhere—once his skull stops splitting apart, anyway.

"Minute," he croaks, his voice rasping in his throat. Vomit tries to rise up, but he suppresses it as ruthlessly as possible—just the thought of vomiting right now and how his head will feel afterward makes him want to cry.

Thankfully Tolly gets it, not speaking again until Mikey lifts a hand to indicate that it's okay. "I called the nurse," he says, still that same soft whisper.

"Concussion, huh?" Mikey manages, swallowing hard against the thought. He didn't even really need to ask the question; head injury plus light sensitivity and nausea is a pretty simple equation, even for someone who almost had to repeat Algebra. Even if he hadn't been here before, which he has. "Shit."

"Probably," Tolly agrees, because he's incapable of lying if someone asks him directly. Well, to Mikey at least. "Stewie went to find a nurse, but it seems like."

Suddenly, brutally aware of the itch on his nose, Mikey lifts his hand to scratch it—or tries to, anyway— and discovers that the heavy, throbbing ache in his right arm wasn't just in his head. It hurts to move his left hand, too, but not as much. After scratching the fucking itch, he reaches over and, yep, that's a cast on his right arm. "Fucking shit. So much for the fucking season."

"Don't worry about the season," Tolly says, because of course he does. "It's still early, but you need to rest right now."

Any protest he might have made is cut off by the door clicking open. "How are you feeling, Mr. Michaelson?" a quiet female voice asks, cool fingers landing on his left wrist.

It takes Mikey a second to realize she's talking to him. Probably the concussion, but maybe the fact that he's been "Mikey" since he started Mites. Who knows. Oh, shit he didn't answer.

"Like someone's hitting me on the head with a hockey stick," he answers honestly.

She hums softly, letting go of his wrist. The tapping of fingers on a keyboard is the next sound, and he can't help wincing. "I'll get you something for the pain, but first we've got to go through the protocol, now that you're awake."

Mikey sighs. "Yeah, I figured."

The nurse—her name is Morgan, apparently—moves through the concussion protocol with an efficiency he'd probably appreciate more if he could concentrate. It seems redundant—obviously he has a concussion—but he answers as best he can. At some point during the process, Tolly's hand brushes against the fingers of Mikey's right hand, anchoring him.

"Well, the doctor will need to see you," Morgan says finally, "but we're definitely keeping you overnight for observation. Home health aides will be checking up on you after release. Do you live alone?"

"I'm his roommate," Tolly speaks up before Mikey can process that. "And his family is driving in. They should be here anytime, actually."

Mikey groans, and immediately regrets it. Catching his breath, waiting for the pain to subside, takes a minute. "You called them? Harsh, bro."

"The front office called them," Tolly corrects. "If you didn't want that, you should've changed your emergency medical contact."

Which is a fair point, not that Mikey's willing to concede it. Just the thought of his parents and sisters crowded into this room makes him feel like his head is going to literally explode. "Can't you keep them out?"

"Hospital policy limits the number of visitors in a room," Morgan answers, even though he wasn't technically asking her. "And you can, of course, ask us to keep everyone out."

"Well, not everybody," he says hastily, whining a little when the throbbing in his head kicks up a notch, scattering his thoughts. It seems to take longer this time. "Tolly can stay. I mean, if you want."

Tolly snorts quietly, squeezing his fingertips gently. "Just try getting rid of me, asshole."

"I'm going to get you some pain meds," Morgan says, completely ignoring their interaction. "The doctor will be by to check on you soon, but in the meantime, use your call button if you need anything."

"Okay," Mikey says faintly, not really sure what he was agreeing to. But that's okay. Tolly's here.

The door clicks open, a soft murmur of voices, then closes again, quiet footsteps crossing toward the bed. "How're you feeling, kiddo?" Stewie asks quietly.

"Like death," Mikey says; he knows it's not going to get better for awhile, but he's already tired of that question. "Did we win at least?"

Silence is his only answer. He wants to kick his feet, to punch someone, but the pain in his head keeps him immobile. "Shit."

"Don't worry about that right now," Stewie says, unconsciously echoing Tolly's words from earlier. "They get you anything for the pain yet?"

As if on cue, the door opens again. Mikey risks cracking an eye open, and yes, it's a woman in scrubs, carrying a syringe. "Thank you," he says, quiet but fervent.

"We'll get you fixed up as fast as we can," she says, crossing to the computer. He recognizes Morgan's voice, watching vaguely as she taps away at the keyboard for a few seconds, then uses a little barcode scanner thing to scan the syringe and his hospital bracelet. "Here we go."

She slides the needle into the little opening on his IV and depresses the plunger. It's probably his imagination, but he thinks he can feel the cool wash of the medication through his veins, every beat of his heart carrying it to the places where he hurts.

"I'll be back to check on you," she says, capping the

syringe and disposing of it in the little red box by the door. "Get some rest if you can."

It's definitely not his imagination now; Mikey's starting to feel that floaty, faraway sensation that tells him she gave him the really good drugs. He can still feel the pain, but it's distant. Unimportant. "'Kay."

Somewhere a phone vibrates, and Tolly makes a noise. "Your family's here, man. You feel up to it?"

Mikey isn't sure, really. He probably feels something. Maybe that something is up to it. "Can you tell them to be really quiet?"

Stewie laughs softly. "Yeah, bud, we can do that. How about I go out and talk to them, let them come in a couple at a time?"

Nodding was a mistake, but sadly Mikey only realizes after the fact. He takes long, deep breaths, trying to keep the nausea and his dinner from making a comeback, waiting for the pleasant fog to come back. "Yeah," he finally says. "Sounds good, Cap."

Thankfully Stewie refrains from his usual hair-ruffling, patting Mikey's arm gently instead before heading out of the room. Tolly makes like he's going to stand, too, and Mikey squeezes his hand as much as he can with the cast, which is honestly pretty pathetic.

"I should let you have your family time," Tolly says, but he settles back in his chair.

"Nah, stay," Mikey says, forming the words slowly and carefully through the soft blur that's settled over his head. "They won't yell as much if you're here."

Tolly shakes his head. "Dude, have you met your parents?" He doesn't try to get up again, though, so Mikey's pretty sure he won that argument.

The next few minutes—or maybe more, he honestly loses track—are kind of a blur. His mom cries a little; he's pretty sure of that, and his dad's eyes are suspiciously wet. Andrea and Diana mock him as usual, even if their insults are a bit more gentle than normal. But everyone is quiet, their hands gentle if they touch him, and Tolly is there.

Finally the nurse comes in and firmly chases everyone out, or Mikey thinks she does. He's drifting in and out at this point, not sure what's a dream and what's really happening. But Tolly's there every time he opens his eyes, so that's okay.

"I DON'T NEED A WHEELCHAIR," Mikey whines. He cringes a little as soon as he hears it—it's definitely a whine —but considering his season's probably over, he thinks he's allowed. "I can walk."

Tolly sighs. "Bro, first of all, you almost fell down walking to the bathroom this morning."

"I was wearing socks and the floor is slippery," Mikey counters. "Could've happened to anybody."

From the look he gets, Tolly is not amused. "Secondly, your mom will drive back here and beat me up if she ever hears that I let you walk out to the car with a concussion. So unless you want to stay here eating shitty hospital food for another day, or be responsible for my death at your mom's hands, get your ass in the wheelchair and let's go home."

"Ugh, fine," Mikey mutters, swinging his legs over the side of the bed and standing up.

It's honestly insulting how hard it is to keep his balance. He's a fucking professional athlete—he can walk four steps from his bed to the stupid wheelchair without falling on his ass.

Probably.

Thankfully Tolly doesn't say anything about the fact that he falls into the wheelchair more than sits, wincing a little at the impact. This is why they're best friends, honestly. Tolly just waits patiently while Mikey gets his feet on the stupid footrests, then gathers up the discharge papers and the little overnight bag of Mikey's stuff his mom had brought over before they drove home.

"Ready?" he asks.

Mikey takes a deep breath. "Yeah, let's get the fuck out of here."

He's pathetically grateful for the wheelchair as soon as they leave his dimly lit room. The brighter lights of the hallway feel like needles stabbing into his eyes before he manages to close them.

"Okay?" Tolly asks softly. He stops for a second, not waiting for an answer, and then something settles on Mikey's nose and over his ears.

It takes him an embarrassingly long time to recognize them as sunglasses. Opening his eyes again as they start to move is a little better, less stabby feeling, but then the vertigo hits and he closes them again, giving up on open eyes for the moment.

"Yeah," Mikey manages, swallowing hard. He refuses to vomit on himself on the way out of the hospital. "Just go."

Tolly takes him at his word, pushing him through the halls and then pausing, probably for the elevator. His suspicion is confirmed when he hears a ding that's probably soft but adds another fun stabby sensation to the throbbing in his head. There's a slight bump as Tolly wheels him over the threshold, then the sinking feeling in his stomach as they head downward.

He's braced for the ding this time. Not that it hurts less that way, but at least it's not a surprise. As Tolly pushes him out of the elevator, he focuses on keeping his eyes closed and his face and neck relaxed, on not tensing up and making it worse. Focusing on what he can hear helps —the footsteps of people around him, the quiet buzz of conversations. The whoosh of automatic doors and colder outside air rushing over him.

"Thanks," Tolly says.

Mikey's momentarily confused, but then he hears Suzie say "No problem, man. How you feeling, Mikey-boy?"

"Like I got hit by the Wendigos' entire d-line," he grumbles, keeping his eyes closed.

"Sucks," Suzie agrees, squeezing his good shoulder gently. "Car's right there, but I gotta get home; Chris is gonna kill me if I leave him alone with the baby any longer. Let us know if you need anything else, okay?"

By the time Mikey manages to parse that, Tolly is already saying, "Will do." There's the backslapping noise of a bro-hug, then Suzie squeezes his shoulder one more time before his footsteps recede and the wheelchair starts moving again.

"Almost there," Tolly says quietly. "Good thing you didn't get that big fuck-off pickup you were looking at. I wouldn't want to pick your ass up after you fell out of that."

"Fuck you," Mikey retorts automatically, but then he thinks about it and yeah, that's a point.

They stop moving then. "Hold on a sec," Tolly says, moving around. There's a weird sound—it takes Mikey a minute to identify it as a car door opening, he's never really paid attention to it before—and then Tolly's hand is on his good elbow.

"Slow and steady," Tolly says, holding on as Mikey gets his feet on the ground. "If you don't want to open your eyes, just let me guide you, okay?"

"Okay," Mikey whispers, taking a deep breath before he stands.

For a second he regrets all his life choices. Surely the light isn't worse than his head spinning from not being able to see, but when he cracks his eyes open, he rethinks that premise. Only Tolly's steady hands, one on his elbow, one on the small of his back, keep him upright.

"Here we go," Tolly says, guiding him toward where

the car had been in that brief flash of vision. "Okay, turn, yeah, like that. And sit down, but watch your head."

Mikey lets himself be guided, too nauseated to worry about anything besides not vomiting. Tolly doesn't seem to mind, getting his legs up inside the car, buckling his seatbelt for him, and closing the door gently.

Even with his eyes closed, the difference in the light is immediate, and Mikey thanks every deity who might be listening that he got the windows tinted, even though his sisters made fun of him at the time. He waits until Tolly slides into the driver's seat and closes the door before opening his eyes again, but between the tint and the sunglasses, it's almost bearable.

"Ready?" he asks, buckling his own seatbelt and hitting the ignition button.

"Home, Jeeves," Mikey manages to joke. It's weak, and they both know it, but the look Tolly sends him says he appreciates the attempt at normal as much as Mikey did.

Putting the car in gear, he pulls slowly out of the circle drive in front of the hospital, accelerating with a smoothness that Mikey appreciates. "Okay," he agrees. "Let's go home."

Three days before preseason

"Granite countertops in the kitchen," the realtor says, like she hasn't figured out that they're 21-year-old professional athletes

who don't give a fuck what their counters are made of. "Professional-grade range and refrigerator, a large living space connected to the kitchen for entertaining. And the building security is top-notch; twenty-four hour concierge service and secure parking. You get two parking spaces with the condo, but you can purchase more if needed."

Mikey exchanges a look with Tolya. "Two should be fine," he says, doing his best to channel his dad. "Can we look at the bedrooms?" That seems like a thing they should do.

"Certainly!" she says, smiling at him like he's a puppy doing a new trick. "Right down this hall. There are dual masters, each with their own full-size bathroom and soaking tub."

Tolya raises his eyebrows as they follow her, and Mikey nods back. The cost of this condo kind of makes him want to stab himself in the eye, and he prays his mom never finds out the exact number. But the building is super close to the arena, and honestly, they don't have a lot of time. Besides, it's not like they can't afford it.

"Can you give us a minute?" Tolya asks after the realtor has shown them around both bedrooms and bathrooms, gushing over the walk-in closets and warming towel racks and whatever the fuck else she thinks they care about.

"Oh, of course. I'll just be in the kitchen making some calls if you think of any other questions."

Mikey waits until the door closes behind her before turning to Tolya, his voice lowered in case the bedrooms aren't soundproof. He should probably ask the realtor about that. "What's up?"

"I don't know." Tolya shoves his hands into his pockets. "It's nice, it's got everything we need, but—what if I get sent down? Or you do?"

Pushing down his instinctive protest, Mikey stops to really consider the possibility, as unlikely as it seems. He doesn't realize he's pacing until Tolya grabs his arm as he passes, stopping him.

"Well," he says slowly. "I don't know the exact details of your contract, but I'm pretty sure I can afford this place on my own if I have to. Which I don't think I will."

Tolya opens his mouth, closes it again. "Okay, yeah," he says. "This is on the high end of what my accountant said I could do, but still doable."

"Besides," Mikey says, wrapping an arm around Tolya's shoulder. "Think positive. We're gonna stay up, we're gonna play our asses off, and we'll live in this place for years."

"Bro," Tolya says, but he's smiling even as he shakes his head, as he lets Mikey pull him toward the bedroom door.

Mikey just smiles back. "Come on. Let's do it."

3

———————

TOLYA

"**I** can do it!" Mikey says, even though he clearly fucking can't.

At this point, Tolya doesn't even bother to hide his rolling eyes. Because, seriously, Mikey is the stubbornest son of a bitch Tolya's ever met, and that includes his dad. The first couple of days weren't so bad, when he was still on the good drugs. But now he's back to Tylenol and ibuprofen, irritable because he's in pain. Plus he keeps forgetting (or pretending to forget) that he can't do everything he used to do, because he has a *broken arm* and a *concussion.*

Making a mental note to text his mom for advice in dealing with stubborn fucking hockey players who don't know their limits, Tolya takes a deep breath. "Look, bro, I don't want to clean up vomit again, okay? Plus you know

Stewie will kill me if he thinks I'm not taking care of you. C'mon, let me help."

"I'm not three," Mikey mutters, but he hands the shorts over instead of bending over again to try and put them on.

"No, you're injured," Tolya shoots back, holding the shorts out for Mikey to step into. "Just…let me, okay? I can't fix your head or your arm, but I can help you get dressed so you don't puke."

Mikey groans, but he lets Tolya pull the shorts up over his hips. "Ugh. Fine, but only because puking is the worst."

Tolya wants to punch him in the shoulder, but remembers he shouldn't at the last minute. "You're the best."

"No, man," Mikey says, his face going serious. "Look, I know I've been super bitchy lately, but I appreciate it. You know you don't have to, though. Andrea or somebody can come stay with me, or there's the home health aides."

"What are friends for?" Tolya says. There's no way he's going to let Mikey fend for himself, not when he's here to help. The aides are super nice and friendly, but he always feels a little weird about them coming over, like his mom is going to fly in from Jersey to smack him if he doesn't clean up before they come or if he forgets to offer them a drink. And Andrea and Diana are pretty cool, like, he wouldn't mind having sisters like them, but the thought of them staying long-term, sleeping on the couch, eating all the snacks, making snide comments—he shudders.

"Seriously," he continues, doing his best to meet Mikey's eyes and show his absolute sincerity. "I don't mind."

Mikey stares into his eyes for several seconds longer than he's been holding eye contact lately. Tolya makes himself stare back.

"Okay," Mikey finally says.

Tolya lets out a breath he didn't realize he was holding. "Okay," he repeats. "How about breakfast. What do you want to throw up today?"

The look he gets in return is supremely unimpressed, but finally Mikey relents. "Bacon?"

"You got it," Tolya tells him, heading for the kitchen. "Come on, I don't trust you not to do something stupid if I leave you alone."

"Wow," Mikey grumbles, but he follows along, so Tolya will take that as a win.

Besides, it's not exactly a hardship to have Mikey hanging out one one of their cushy barstools while he cooks. The kitchen is dim, thanks to the blackout shades Tolya had paid a ridiculous amount to get installed in a rush, but the little light over the stove shows him enough to lay strips of bacon across the cast-iron griddle his mom had insisted on buying him when he moved out. He really needs to remember to thank her next time they talk.

"Hey," Mikey says.

Tolya looks up, pulled out of his reverie. "What's up?"

"Just—" Mikey shakes his head. Tolya can't be sure in

the dim light, but it looks like his cheeks are a little red. "Thanks."

"Anytime," Tolya tells him, turning back to the stove.

"Shit!" Mikey yells, his curses accompanied by a loud clattering noise from the kitchen.

Tolya is off the couch before he even realizes he's moved. All he can see from the living area is Mikey's back, his shoulders slumped. When he rounds the corner of the bar, though, he can see the whole picture. The plate on the floor. The pasta, some of it still on the plate, but most of it spattered across the floor, the cabinet doors, and Mikey's sweatpants and t-shirt.

"I—fuck," Mikey grinds out, his free hand coming up to his head.

"Come on," Tolya says, making an executive decision. "Let's get you some clean clothes and then I'll heat up your lunch. It's almost time for some Tylenol."

Mikey clenches his jaw, then winces more. But he doesn't fight when Tolya leads him toward his room, so that's something.

Tolya barely hears the rattling noise—honestly if he hadn't been listening closely, he probably wouldn't have noticed it. But seriously, Mikey's only been home from the hospital for a few days. Sure, he smells a little rank, but he still gets dizzy spells. Showering, alone, where he could fall and crack his idiot head open—again—is a terrible idea.

Unfortunately, even though Tolya spent the entire time he was taping a plastic bag over the cast explaining this, Mikey decided to dig in his heels and insist on showering alone. So maybe Tolya found something so interesting on his phone that he ended up leaning against the wall outside the bathroom door. Maybe he burst through the bathroom door as soon as he heard the rattle and thump. Possibly.

"Goddamn it, Tolly," Mikey says through gritted teeth, but he's slumped against the glass shower enclosure, his eyes closed.

"Bro," Tolya says, stripping off his shirt as he crosses the bathroom. "If you give yourself another concussion, literally everyone will be lining up to kick my ass. Including me. Don't make me have to kick my own ass."

Mikey sighs so loudly it's audible even over the sound of the shower. "Dude, I fucking reek. I can feel my skin crawling with how gross it is. I just want to be clean."

"I know." Tolya finishes taking his clothes off. "Move over so I can come in."

"Dude, what?"

Tolya rolls his eyes. "We shower like ten feet apart most days, max, it's not like I've never seen your dick. You want to be clean, I want you not to fall down. Just pretend I'm not here."

Mikey splutters, but he does shift over so Tolya can

pull the door open and step into the shower stall. "Dude—"

"Just pretend I'm not here," Tolya says, leaning against the tile, close enough to grab Mikey if he starts to slip. He does his best to keep his eyes firmly at chest level or above, sort of unfocused. It shouldn't be this difficult, honestly. He's been sharing locker room showers with other people since he was old enough to play, but this is different somehow. Maybe it's the close quarters, or the fact that this is a home shower and not the wide-open space of a locker room. Whatever it is though, it feels strange enough that he can't quite settle, shifting restlessly.

After a second, Mikey reaches for the washcloth and his body wash, then makes a frustrated noise when he realizes he only has one functioning hand to use.

"Want me to—"

"No," Mikey grits out. He manages to drape the washcloth over his casted hand so he can squeeze the body wash onto it. He puts the body wash back on the shelf carefully, then grabs the washcloth with his free hand and starts clumsily lathering himself up.

Tolya jerks his eyes upward when they start following the path of the washcloth down Mikey's torso. There's something terribly domestic about this that doesn't happen when they're in the showers after practice. It's…intimate. Yeah, sure, he and Mikey are close—PR has really been pushing that narrative and there's been a bajillion puff pieces about their "bromance," which isn't entirely inaccurate.

But something about the situation, the steamy air of the shower, the shower that's objectively large but feels suddenly cramped with two professional athletes crammed into it, the way Tolya's suddenly aware of Mikey's body, not as a thing to function for the team, but an aesthetic object, the flex and play of his muscles as he strains to clean as much of himself as he can—

He's so lost in thought that he almost misses it when Mikey leans over to scrub at his legs and starts to wobble, then tip over. Tolya catches him under the arms and hauls him upright. Mikey takes a stumbling step trying to catch his balance, but his weight on Tolya is enough to push them both backward.

Thankfully the shower wall stops them, the cold tile shocking against Tolya's back in contrast with the warm, steamy air. It's a welcome distraction, though, because Mikey's body is plastered against his. Mikey's naked, wet body.

Tolya's cock takes this moment to remind him that he hasn't gotten laid in awhile, and that he's been too stressed and tired the past few days for more than a cursory jerk-off session. His cock is the literal worst.

"Sorry," Mikey says, his voice soft and a little breathy and definitely *not helping*.

"What I'm here for," Tolya says, as much to remind himself as to remind Mikey. He nudges Mikey back onto his feet, holding on around his ribcage until Mikey's steady before letting go. "Let me get your legs, okay? Seriously, not worth another concussion."

Mikey swallows, his face even pinker than before. "It —don't worry about it. The soap'll rinse down. It'll be fine."

Tolya considers protesting, but kneeling at Mikey's feet to scrub his legs is almost certainly a bridge too far if they're going to keep this from reaching bad-porno levels. "Okay. What about your hair?"

"Oh yeah."

Mikey backs into the spray and tips his head back, eyes closing as he lets the water slick his thick, dark hair back. The noise he makes is maybe the least helpful thing for Tolya's stupid cock, now half-hard and really taking an interest in the proceedings.

He spares a moment to be grateful he's not eighteen anymore, or he'd already be at full salute, and does his best to think of disgusting things. The smell of his pads after practice, the grayish-green glop that the cafeteria used to serve for lunch in third grade, the splatter of blood on the ice when Mikey went down.

Eventually Mikey stops making porn noises under the showerhead and reaches for the shampoo, only to discover there's no way he can squeeze it into his good hand. "Motherfucker!"

"Here," Tolya says, taking it from him. Mikey holds out his hand, but Tolya ignores him, pouring shampoo into his own hand and setting it aside. "Turn around."

Mikey gives him a skeptical look but does as he's told. It's probably a bad idea, Tolya tells himself. He should put the shampoo in Mikey's hand, let him take care of himself.

Instead, he rubs his hands together until they're coated in a thick, creamy lather, then lifts them to work it through Mikey's hair, massaging his scalp as firmly as he dares.

"Fuck," Mikey groans, tipping his head back into Tolya's hands. "God, you have no idea how good that feels."

"I broke my wrist in Juniors," Tolya replies, making sure to get every inch of Mikey's scalp. "After a week I was about ready to shave my head. My billet mom took me to her salon and I thought I'd died and gone to heaven."

Mikey laughs, the little snorting chuckle that Tolya would chirp him for if it wasn't so adorable. "Well, if hockey doesn't pan out, you've got a second career all lined up."

Tolya pulls his hands free reluctantly, pinching him gently on the bicep before rinsing his hands clean. "Knock on fucking wood when you say that, bro. You're good here, rinse it out."

On the one hand, now he doesn't have to listen to Mikey sounding like sex while Tolya's touching him. On the other hand, now he can see the expression of bliss on Mikey's face as he turns his head under the water, running his free hand through his hair to make sure it's rinsed clean. Now he can wonder if—

He slams a mental door shut on that line of speculation. Nothing good can come of it. "Conditioner?"

"Yeah," Mikey agrees, blinking his eyes open, and shit,

he has water drops on his eyelashes. Fuck. Now is *not the time.*

He probably should rush them toward finishing, Tolya thinks, but apparently he has an unexpected masochistic streak. Because instead he takes even more time than he did with the shampoo, making sure the conditioner is evenly distributed through Mikey's hair, then massaging his scalp until his fingers are sore.

"This is always the most boring part," Mikey says after a minute, his voice soft and dreamy. "Waiting until time to rinse it out. But seriously, dude, thank you."

"Whatever you need," Tolya says absently, reaching over Mikey's shoulders to rinse the conditioner off his hands. "Concussions fucking suck."

Mikey sighs. "They really fucking do. And like, I don't even like to think about needing my mom to help with this, you know?"

Tolya nods, then remembers that Mikey's back is turned to him. "Yeah, for sure."

He has no idea how long they stand there in strangely comfortable silence, his stupid cock notwithstanding, but eventually Mikey sighs and moves away, rinsing the conditioner out and turning off the water.

"Gimme a sec," Tolya orders, sliding the door open and grabbing a towel. He's not really that wet, since he was out of the spray, just a little on his feet and legs, and his hands. Some remaining droplets where Mikey had landed against him—nope, not thinking about that right now.

It only takes a few seconds to dry himself off and wrap

a towel around his waist. He grabs another one and holds it out to Mikey, who takes it with a scowl.

"I can—"

"If you say you can do it yourself, I'm going—" Tolya pauses, trying to think of a sufficiently severe consequence. "I'm gonna text Andrea and tell her you almost fell in the shower."

Mikey pouts at him. It shouldn't be adorable. "That's just wrong, dude."

Tolya shrugs. "Whatever it takes. First priority is keeping you in one piece."

"Fine," Mikey growls, drying as much of himself as he can reach, as slowly as possible. He doesn't bend down to get his legs, though. Tolya will take it.

He doesn't think about the inevitable consequences of his action until he's dried Mikey's back and is kneeling on the fluffy bath mat, rubbing the towel over his legs. His cock is completely on board with this, bobbing against his towel in a way he can only hope isn't super obvious. Breathing through his nose, as slowly as possible, he does his best to think unsexy thoughts.

Like, objectively, Mikey's feet are kind of gross. His legs are nice, sure, muscles shifting under the surface, especially his thighs and—nope, not going any higher. But he's got the weird knobby ankles and feet that pretty much every player has—Tolya saw an article about why, once, and trying to remember the details gets him through this without embarrassing himself. Hopefully.

"There you go," he says, handing the towel up to

Mikey and gathering his clothes off the floor, not standing until his back is turned. Just in case. "Give me a sec and I can help you get dressed."

Mikey starts to protest, but when Tolya shoots him a look over his shoulder, he closes his mouth. "Fine."

"Fine," Tolya repeats, dropping his towel after only a slight hesitation and pulling his boxers back on. They were just naked in the shower together; it's dumb to feel awkward about dressing in front of Mikey. "You have clean clothes?"

"In my room," Mikey says, brushing past him and heading toward the door. "If I can walk there without supervision."

Tolya rolls his eyes and bites his tongue to hold back the words that want to escape. Mikey's tired and hurting and facing the likelihood of his season being over. It's not fair to expect him to be his normal cheerful self.

But he's seriously the worst patient ever.

TOLYA's not rushing home from practice—okay, he's rushing, but leaving Mikey home alone had him jumpy and distracted all through practice, even though the home health aides were supposed to check in on him partway through. But some part of him isn't going to believe that Mikey's okay until he sees it with his own two eyes.

He barely restrains himself from bursting into the apartment, turning the knob and pushing the door open as quietly as he can. It's dark, even compared to the overcast light outside, so it takes his eyes a minute to adjust.

As soon as he makes out Mikey huddled on the couch, clutching at his head, he might actually teleport across the room; one second he's standing just inside the door, the next thing he knows, he's kneeling by the couch, resting a tentative hand on Mikey's knee.

"Hurts," Mikey says, his voice muffled by his hands.

"I'll grab you some Tylenol," Tolya whispers, cringing a little when Mikey winces at even that much noise. Thankfully, the Tylenol is on the end table, along with a bottle of water—and Mikey's phone, which he's not supposed to have. "Dude."

Mikey flinches at the increased volume, but takes the pills and water when Tolya hands them over. Moving his head enough to swallow them leaves him shaking by the end of it, so Tolya helps him lie down. Berating him can wait until he doesn't look so breakable. Probably.

Tolya has a sneaking feeling he needs to get used to being a soft touch where Mikey's concerned.

After first regular season game

"Come on," Mikey says, steering them back toward the center of the hallway just in time for Tolya's hair to barely brush against the wall instead of his head thunking into it. "Almost there."

"Y'r the best," Tolya says, or tries to say. It sounds different outside his head. "'Ja know that?"

Mikey shoves Tolya's door open with his foot, a feat of balance that Tolya can only watch in awe. "You might have mentioned it. Fourteen or fifteen times."

"Why aren'cha drunk?" Tolya demands plaintively, but allows Mikey to steer him toward his bed. He just means to sit down, but the room won't stop moving. Lying down is better. Even if something keeps pulling at his legs. When he finally figures out how to lift his head and look, Mikey is unlacing his shoes and taking them off. What a bro. "Y'r the best."

"Thank you," Mikey says, setting the second shoe down and swinging Tolya's legs up onto the bed. "And I'm not drunk because I don't like puking, which is what you're going to be doing tomorrow."

Tolya shakes his head and immediately regrets it. "Nah," he says, closing his eyes again. "'M Russian. Russians don't get hangov'rs."

"Sure." Mikey pats his shin and pushes to his feet. "How about I get you a bottle of water and some Tylenol for the morning, just in case."

"Okay." Tolya can't imagine wanting to argue with Mikey right now. Or with anyone. He played his first regular season CHL game, he's got a great friend and d-partner. Everything is warm and fuzzy and good. "It's good."

When he wakes up in the morning, still in his game day shirt and slacks, head pounding, mouth tasting like something died in it, he nearly cries when he sees the Tylenol and the water on his bedside table.

4

MIKEY

Mikey is *bored.*

He knows, objectively, that he's being terrible to live with. Honestly, he's kind of surprised that Tolly hasn't gone storming out of the apartment or gotten a hotel room or something just to not have to deal with his shit. But seriously, this being injured shit is the worst. Especially with a concussion.

He can't watch TV; back in college when he had a concussion, he'd managed to convince his roommate that he would just listen to the show. The vomiting after he forgot he wasn't supposed to be watching was epic enough to sear itself into his memory. So, no TV.

And he can't use his phone, even a little bit. No texting, no Snapchat, no Youtube videos of cute animals or elaborate food he's never going to cook, no cute dogs to add to his Insta. Listening to sports radio involves enough discussion of hockey in general and Mikey's injury in particular that Tolly vetoes it after about an hour. And all the music stations make his head hurt worse, even if they weren't super repetitive.

"Here," Tolly says one morning before practice, handing him a battered iPod.

"Dude, I can't—"

Tolly shakes his head, cutting Mikey off. "It's not music. I downloaded some podcasts and some audiobooks for you to listen to while I'm at practice. So you don't do something stupid, like try to fuck with your phone again."

Mikey sighs. "Well, I can't, because you hid my phone. But, uh, thanks."

"I wouldn't put it past you to find it if you were bored enough," Tolly says darkly. "Anyway, I got a bunch of episodes of The Adventure Zone and Welcome to Night Vale, plus the audiobooks for the new Rick Riordan series, because you keep bitching that you don't have enough time to read them. What do you want me to start for you?"

"Uh, probably one of the podcasts," Mikey says, giving the iPod back.

Tolly fiddles with it for a few seconds, then plugs it into a set of speakers on the coffee table. "There. Need anything else before I go?"

"Nah," Mikey says. He honestly thinks he might cry a little once he's alone; this might be the nicest thing anyone's ever done for him. "I'm good. Thanks."

"Just press play when you're ready to start," Tolly says, slinging his bag onto his shoulder. "Don't do anything stupid while I'm gone, okay?"

Mikey bites his lip on the perfect retort, because Tolly's being super patient about all of his shit. And even if he'd definitely recognize the line from Captain America, now isn't a good time to tell him he's taking the stupid with him. He's not the one with a concussion here, or the one who tried to use his phone with a concussion. "Okay," he replies.

The door shuts behind Tolly with a soft click instead of his usual slam, of course, because Tolly is fucking thoughtful and awesome and a great bro. Mikey appreciates it, he really does. It's just that he also has the childish impulse to poke at that wall of patience, to find out what it'll take to make him snap.

But he's not ten anymore, jabbering at Andrea and Diana, doing everything he can to get them to react. He's twenty-one years old, living on his own, a professional athlete. He can control himself. And he will.

He presses play and settles back on the couch, closing his eyes, because why not? It's not like there's anything for him to look at, and once he gets caught up enough with what's happening in the podcast, he's distracted enough to not focus on the slight, perpetual throb in his head.

Despite how interested he is in the story, he must drift off at some point, only waking up when the door clicks open hours later, signaling Tolly's return.

"Good practice?" he asks sleepily, reaching over to hit

pause on the iPod. He'll have to figure out where he fell asleep eventually, but not now.

"It was okay," Tolly says, running a hand through his still-damp hair. "You hungry? I'm gonna make lunch."

Now that he mentions it, Mikey's stomach is feeling a little hollow. "I could eat," he says, sitting up cautiously, then getting to his feet once he's sure the room isn't going to revolve around him.

"I can make sandwiches without supervision," Tolly says dryly when Mikey joins him.

"Yeah, I know," Mikey says, edging onto the barstool he usually uses to watch Tolly cook. "But it's more fun when I can bug you."

Tolly rolls his eyes. "Great."

"Everything's more fun with you," Mikey says, and oops, that came out a little more sincere than he was planning. Stupid concussion, making him have feelings all over the place. "Anyway, what'd you do in practice? Anything interesting? Who's Coach got you paired with?"

"They called a guy up from Bakersfield," Tolly says after a long moment of side-eye. "I guess he played with Sunshine in college? Pretty solid, but we're still getting used to each other."

It takes a little more prodding, but eventually Tolly's mostly talking without prompting, telling him about the dumb, everyday things that happen every practice. Normally Mikey wouldn't think twice about this kind of shit, but now he can feel his throat getting tight at the mention of Plats and Suzie competing to see who can bounce the most shots off someone's skates, or how surprised the new trainer was when she walked in on Tiger doing his naked goalie stretches.

Fortunately that's about the point where Tolly finishes their sandwiches, sliding Mikey's in front of him along with a glass of water and a couple of Ibuprofen. He slides onto the barstool next to Mikey and finishes his story in between bites, their knees bumping together. It's not as good as eating at the arena, as actually getting to be there, but it's better than being alone.

Everything really is better with Tolly.

"Hey," Tolly says that night, around the time that he'd normally head to bed. "I, uh, got you something when I was out."

"Present? Gimme!" Mikey says, because yeah, he's injured, and even when he isn't, he doesn't have a lot of shame.

Rolling his eyes, Tolly digs around in his bag and pulls out—

"A book?" Mikey looks up at him, confused. This seems rude and not at all like Tolly. "Dude, you know I can't—"

Tolly ducks his head and wow, is he blushing? "I, uh, I thought I could read it to you? Like, not all at once, but a chapter at a time. You said you were having trouble getting to sleep, and you keep talking about catching up on all the Discworld books you missed in Juniors."

"Awww," Mikey grins, unable to help himself. "Are you gonna read me a bedtime story?"

"Shut the fuck up," Tolly mutters, definitely blushing now. "It's dumb, I'll take it back—

Mikey yelps. "No, don't! That sounds really fucking awesome, dude. Seriously, above and beyond the call of duty."

Tolly shrugs, but he doesn't put *Night Watch* back in his bag. "Well, I wanted to read it too, so."

"Sweet." Mikey pats the cushion next to him, waiting until Tolly sits down before stretching out, grabbing his favorite throw blanket, and tucking his toes under Tolly's leg—his toes are cold, okay? And Tolly always runs warm. "Okay, I'm ready."

"Are you sure?" Tolly asks, raising his eyebrows. "You want a pillow or a glass of warm milk first?"

Mikey jabs upward with his toes, although it probably hurts him more than it hurts Tolly, given that Tolly's thighs are like fucking granite. "C'mon, please?"

Whether it was the jab or the puppy-dog eyes that do it, Tolly finally opens the book, turning on the lamp on the side table and adjusting the shade so it's shining on the page and not in Mikey's eyes, flipping through the stuff at the front until he finds the first chapter. Clearing his throat a little self-consciously, he glances over at Mikey, then back at the page.

"Chapter One. Sam Vimes sighed when he heard the scream…"Tolly began, his eyes moving over the page.

Mikey lets himself drift, half-listening, half watching Tolly's face, the way his mouth shapes the words, the way it quirks up at the corners when he's amused by what he's reading, which is most of the time.

He realizes, with a not-entirely-unpleasant tilting feeling in his stomach, that Tolly is really hot. Or well, maybe realizes isn't the best word. He's seen Tolly's face every day since they've moved in together; at this point, it might be more familiar to him than his own. He knows Tolly is good-looking. Except he's never really looked at him. Or maybe he's never let himself look at him, not while he's sober and fully in control of himself.

Not like he's looking now.

Tolly's lashes are criminally long, leaving shadows on his cheekbones. His stubble is always dark at this time of day—"My Russian winter fur," he always jokes, like he wasn't born in Chicago—but this is the first time Mikey's gotten lost in thought wondering what it would feel like on his neck, or between his thighs—

He jumps when Tolly's hand lands on his shin, big and warm and oh fuck, red alert, abort, abort—

"Hey," Tolly says. "You okay?"

"Yeah." Mikey thinks his voice sounds normal, but maybe it doesn't? He doesn't dare look down at his lap to see if his half-chub is visible, grateful he covered up with the blanket before they got started. "Just a little more tired than I thought I was, I guess. I keep drifting off."

Tolly squeezes gently before lifting his hand. "You wanna head to bed? We can try again tomorrow night."

"Probably oughta," Mikey agrees.

It's harder to force himself to move than it should be, even with the rush of potential humiliation to motivate him. Sitting on the couch, with his feet tucked under Tolly's leg, is warm and comfortable. He doesn't want to leave, to go back to his room and his bed, all alone.

But he has to, unless he wants to have an awkward roommate conversation about why he popped a boner listening to Tolly read a Discworld book. Somehow he manages to swing his legs to the floor while keeping the shielding blanket in place, wrapping it around his waist kind of like a towel.

And that thought reminds him of that shower, of Tolly on his knees on the bath mat, drying him off—

Fuck.

"Stealing the blanket? Seriously?" Tolly asks.

"I got it all warm, and my bed is cold," Mikey replies, not turning around as he walks carefully toward his room. "Grab another one from the chest if you want one."

Tolly sighs. "I guess you *are* injured."

"Damn right," Mikey says, grabbing a trailing blanket edge before it can trip him up. As Tolly keeps reminding him, the last thing he needs is another head injury on top of his concussion. "Night."

"See you in the morning," Tolly replies.

Mikey breathes a sigh of relief once he makes it to his room, the door safely shut behind him. He almost turns the lock, but the mental image of being trapped in his room, needing help and Tolly not being able to get in, stops his hand from moving. Better to run the slight risk of potential embarrassment than the much higher risk of hurting himself while doing something stupid and forcing Tolly to break the door down.

As usual, getting out of his clothes is a struggle, but there's no way in hell he's going to call Tolly for help. Not now. So he fumbles through it, finally crawling under the covers in just his boxers with a sigh of relief.

Whether because it's the first one since his injuries, or because he's got Tolly on the brain, his erection hasn't flagged at all. If anything, he's harder now, his cock tenting the fabric of his boxers, the sheet and blanket he pulled over himself.

He hesitates for a second before reaching for his desk drawer, years of experience telling him not to do this with the door unlocked. But Tolly's really good about knocking before he comes in, and it's been way too long since the last time he was able to jerk off.

Getting the lube out of the drawer is difficult, his left hand clumsy, but he finally manages. Of course, then there's the struggle to get it open, and squeeze it into his palm. By the time he's ready, lube dribbled across his stomach, his cock has gone a little soft, but it still feels really fucking good when he gets his hand around it.

He does his best not to think of anyone in particular as he strokes, but his mind doesn't want to cooperate. It doesn't help that he has to concentrate more to use his left hand; he's always been extremely right-handed, not very good at doing anything with his left. Jerking off with his right became instinctive long ago, just a matter of muscle memory while he watches porn or slips into a fantasy. But now he has to think about how he's moving his hand, when to twist over the head, how tightly to grip. And his stupid left hand just does not want to cooperate.

Between the clumsy motion that just isn't quite hitting where he needs it to and his brain's persistent attempts to associate Tolly with sexual things, he just can't quite get there. He figured it would take longer than usual, but when the lube starts drying out and he's not even close, he gives up. Waiting for his erection to go down on its own is less frustrating at this point than the fits and starts of his clumsy strokes. Maybe it'll be better when he's recovered enough to watch porn again.

Maybe.

Moving night

"Your cousin?" Mikey can't decide whether or not to laugh, because Tolly's story is objectively terrible but also kind of funny, in a dark way.

"Right?" Tolly takes another swig of his beer. "It's not like I'm straight. But I'm not interested in a threesome with my cousin."

Mikey nods, because really, who would be. "Yeah, me

either. I mean, I don't really have many cousins. But, uh, the not straight thing."

Tolly offers a fist and Mikey bumps it in return, unreasonably proud when he manages to do it. He's not that drunk. Probably.

"So what about you?" Tolly asks. "What's your weirdest sex-related story?"

Mikey has to stop and think for a second before it comes back in a flash. "Oh, God. Okay. I didn't do Juniors, so I don't know how weird it got there, but there was this guy on the team back at BU who was always watching porn in the common room. And not like normal porn, you know? Like, sometimes you weren't sure it was actually porn, but anyway—"

He can't quite keep from going off on tangents as he tells the story, but Tolly laughs in all the right places anyway. Sharing an apartment was a good idea for the team, but Mikey's realizing more and more that it's just a good idea in general. He and Tolly just fit.

It's a good thing Mikey learned long ago that teammates and crushes don't mix. It would be so easy to crush on Tolly, the way he always tries to take care of people and do nice things for them. But Mikey's smarter than that.

Really.

5

———

TOLYA

"**Y**ou have my number? And—"

"And your captain's number, and your other captain's number, and his mom's number, and his sister's number," Damon the nurse says, his tone clearly indicating that his patience is wearing thin. "I got this. Go on, kick some Seattle ass. I'll make sure Mr. Michaelson stays in one piece while you're gone."

Tolya ducks his head. "Sorry."

"Get the fuck out of here, dude," Mikey says, not raising his head off the couch. "If you're late to the airport, you're gonna mope for the whole flight and you know it. Go win a damn game."

"Fine," Tolya huffs. "I'm going."

He takes one look back as he heads out the door.

Mikey grins back at him, the last thing he sees before the door closes between them.

Despite Mikey's complaints, he makes it to the airport in plenty of time, not even the last guy on the shuttle from the parking deck to the terminal. While they're waiting for Tiger and Suzie to show up, he has plenty of time to pull his phone out and text Damon. *did I tell you to keep an ear out while he's in the shower?*

Yes. Tolya winces slightly at the punctuation, the implied impatience. *You also told me that he can't use his phone, or watch TV. I have met concussion patients before, you know? I have a nursing degree, even.*

Sorry, Tolya sends back. *He's just stupid and stubborn.*

This time Damon includes a line of eye-rolling emojis before any words, which is probably not standard home nursing aide protocol, but weirdly makes Tolly feel better. *You don't say. Seriously, I got this.*

"Tolly!"

The sound of Lindy's voice finally drags his attention away from his phone. Looking up, Tolya is surprised to see that the bus is stopped at the terminal, empty of everyone except them. "You coming?" Lindy asks, his eyebrows raised in the look that makes him such a good assistant captain, probably learned with his kids.

"Yeah, sorry," Tolya says, shoving his phone in his pocket and grabbing his messenger bag.

"Everything okay with Mikey?" Lindy asks, following him off the bus and into the terminal.

Tolya shrugs. "Yeah, I think so. The doctors aren't

worried. He's just such a dumb shit, I'm pretty sure he's gonna do something stupid and be the first guy in history to get two concussions at the same time."

"I don't think that's medically possible," Lindy says skeptically.

"If anybody could find a way," Tolya says darkly, "It'd be Mikey."

Lindy just laughs, slapping him on the back like he thinks it's a joke. They all think it's a joke. Even Damon doesn't take him seriously, although Tolya thinks after a day or two with Mikey, he'll be singing a different tune.

Tolya files onto the plane with the rest of the team, torn between worry for Mikey and looking forward to saying "I told you so" when he inevitably does something stupid and hurts himself worse. Settling into his usual seat, he suppresses the pang of resentment when his new d-partner sits down next to him. Seth, who got nicknamed "Lightning" for some dumbass reason, is a perfectly nice guy, and a decent player who'll probably be good enough to play in the CHL permanently in another season or two.

It's not his fault he isn't Mikey.

"How's Mikey doing?" Seth asks, further proving that he's a nice guy and doesn't deserve the amount of resentment Tolya feels toward him. Even if that question is getting really fucking old.

Tolya shrugs. "Concussions, man."

"The worst," Seth agrees. He plugs his earbuds into his iPad, tucks his bag under the seat in front of him.

Fortunately for Tolya's desire not to have to

answer the same questions over and over—he loves his team, but they're the nosiest bastards he's ever played with, for all they act like they never check the fucking group chat—the pilot takes that moment to announce that they need to get seated and buckle up for takeoff.

He checks his seatbelt reflexively, even though he buckled it as soon as he sat down, turns his phone to airplane mode, and plugs in his own earbuds. It's a short flight to Seattle, just long enough that he can come up with a decent reason to text Damon again. Probably.

"WHAT NOW?" Damon asks when he answers the phone.

Tolya chooses to ignore the weary tone, which is honestly well-deserved, still riding high on their win over the Selkies even though they're out of the arena and on a bus to the airport. "Can you put it on speaker so I can talk to Mikey, please?"

Damon sighs. "Only because you got the game-winner."

"And it was fucking sweet," he hears Mikey say faintly in the background.

"You only know that because I told you," Damon replies.

Before Tolya can react to that, the sound changes to the tinny quality of a speakerphone call. "Here you go," Damon says.

"Tolly!" Mikey's the only person Tolya's ever met who can yell at low volumes. "You won!"

"We won," Tolya agrees, something in his chest unknotting at the pure joy in Mikey's voice. "How are you doing? Everything okay?"

He can practically hear Mikey rolling his eyes. "Dude. I'm fine. Nothing new here. I swear I haven't done anything stupid, and Damon will back me up. But let's talk about that game! It sounded killer!"

"You listened? Or—"

"Yeah, Damon watched on his phone and told me what was happening when I couldn't figure it out from the commentary. I'm so fucking proud of you, dude! Tell Lightning I said good job!"

It's Tolya's turn to roll his eyes. "First of all, where did that nickname even come from, and secondly, how did you hear about it? It makes no sense!"

"It makes total sense," Mikey retorts. "Seth Carson, Cars, Lightning McQueen from Cars. And just because I can't use my phone doesn't mean I don't hear things."

"Whatever." Tolya's about a hundred and ten percent sure the answer to that question will just annoy him, so he lets it go. They won. Damon's there to deal with whatever dumb shit Mikey's pulling. "I gotta go, we're almost to the airport, but if you think you'll be up, I'll call you when we get to the hotel."

Mikey laughs softly. "Oooh, two phone calls in one day. You sure know how to make a boy feel special."

"Shut up," Tolya says, his cheeks heating. Thankfully

the bus is dark enough that no one on the team will see. Probably. But he almost doesn't care, because he hasn't heard Mikey really laugh since before the concussion. "If you don't want your bedtime story—"

"No, no," Mikey interrupts. "You left me on a cliffhanger last night, asshole, you better not make me wait until tomorrow night."

Tolya opens his mouth to reply, but Trout crashes down into the seat next to him. "Mikey on phone? Mikey! We win!"

"Yeah!" Mikey laughs. "Good job, buddy!"

"Tolya miss you much!" Trout yells, leaning over Tolya to speak directly into the phone. "Like sad puppy without friend! Us too! See soon!"

Tolya gives Trout his best death glare, throwing a vicious elbow to get him to back off. Unfortunately it's too late; the laughter goes out of Mikey's voice, and it's quieter when he replies. "Yeah, see you soon."

Go away, Tolya mouths, shoving Trout until he takes the hint and leaves. "We're almost to the airport now, but I'll call you in a couple hours, okay? Will you still be awake?"

"I'll nap until then," Mikey says, his voice still a little uncertain, but happier. "Don't stand me up, okay?"

"No way. Go nap," Tolya says, turning toward the window like that offers any privacy. "I'll talk to you later."

When he hangs up and settles back into his seat, Stewie is smiling at him from across the aisle. "I'm glad Mikey's got you to look after him."

Tolya shrugs and does his best not to blush again. "He'd do the same for me."

"Yeah," Stewie agrees.

They pull to a stop at the airport terminal before Tolya has to come up with another response. It's probably just as well.

TOLYA DROPS his bag at the foot of the nearest bed in his hotel room, digging his phone out of his pocket and twisting back and forth to try and work out the ache in his lower back after the game, two shuttle bus rides and one plane trip. It's not that late in LA, but Edmonton is an hour earlier so he opts to text Damon rather than call. *He still awake?*

He set an alarm to be sure, is the near-instantaneous response. *He says hurry up*

Grinning, Tolya loosens his tie and digs the copy of Night Watch out of his bag. He wants to call right now, but common sense tells him he should get comfortable now and not have to interrupt the story later. *I'll call in ten.*

It takes him more like five to strip down to his boxer briefs, take a piss, wash his hands, and get settled in the bed with the book and his phone. The bedside lamp casts a warm pool of light over him, the pillows are just firm enough, the sheets crisp and cool agains this skin, and it feels so fucking good to be horizontal that Tolya kind of just wants to go to sleep right now.

But no matter how tired his body is, his brain is still buzzing; there's no way he's going to be able to sleep anytime soon. And besides, he's gotten just as attached to this little bedtime ritual as Mikey has. So he picks up the book and his phone and hits the dial button.

"Hey," Mikey says, his voice tinny over the speaker, but still soft and half-asleep sounding. "You at the hotel?"

"Yeah, all tucked in." Tolya finds himself speaking in the same soft tone. It's all too easy to imagine that Mikey's there with him, in the empty bed just a few feet away. "You ready?"

Covers rustle through the phone. "Yeah, I'm ready."

"Let me put the phone on speaker so I have both hands." Hitting the speaker button and setting the phone on his chest so it can still pick up his voice, Tolya opens the book to his bookmark, a Chipotle receipt folded in half, smiling at the memory of the way Mikey had chirped him for it. "Okay, let's see."

He finds the start of the next chapter and starts to read, losing himself in the story. It's a shock when he comes to the end of the chapter to find himself alone in the hotel room.

"Aw," Mikey complains, his voice slurring a little with sleepiness. "I can't believe he ended the chapter there."

"I know," Tolya agrees, his jaw cracking on a yawn. "I want to keep reading, but my eyes are about to close."

Mikey laughs. "Go to sleep, dude. And don't tell

Coach I'm the reason you stayed up so late or he'll bag-skate me when I come back."

Tolya winces. "Yeah, good point. Okay, I'm going now. You get some sleep, too."

"All I do is sleep," Mikey complains, but the way he loses the last word in a yawn betrays him.

"That's how you heal, dumbass," Tolya says gently, setting the book down on the bedside table and turning off the light. "I'm hanging up now. Sleep, or I'm texting your sisters that you're lonely."

He can almost see the way Mikey shudders at the threat, the wide, betrayed look in his eyes. "Jesus, fine. You don't have to be mean about it."

"Good night, Mikey."

"Night, Tolly. Sweet dreams."

As usual these days, when Tolya comes into the apartment, it's dim, but Mikey's not on the couch, or in the kitchen. At least, he's not visible in the kitchen. *Don't panic,* he tells himself. Unfortunately, he's a dumbass who doesn't listen too good advice.

Dropping his bags by the door, he heads deeper into the apartment. There's no Mikey lying on the kitchen floor in a puddle of his own blood or vomit, much to his relief. The bathroom door is open, the room itself dark and empty.

The door to Mikey's room is cracked just a little, not

enough to see inside. Tolya pushes it open carefully, trying to be quiet, and takes a few steps inside, blinking to try and force his eyes to adjust.

An obnoxious buzz-saw of a snore makes him jump about a foot in the air, but when he comes back down he feels like laughing in relief. He can just barely make out Mikey's sleeping figure now, covers kicked to the foot of the bed, sprawled out on his stomach in only a pair of boxers, his arms wrapped around his pillow. Even as he watches, Mikey shifts, the fingers of his casted hand twitching, his legs moving restlessly over the sheets.

Tolya slips back out as quietly as he can, closing the door most of the way behind him. Mikey's fine. Every loud, obnoxious snore is testament to that fact.

He hadn't realized how tense he was, how worried, until it bleeds out of his muscles, leaving him limp with relief. Walking softly, he makes his way to the couch, settling back against the cushions. He kind of wants a beer, but he's too relaxed to move.

He falls asleep like that, to the rhythm of Mikey's snores.

First roadie of the season

"Are you asleep?"

The whisper is barely audible. Tolya wants to be annoyed,

but honestly, if he'd been asleep it wouldn't have come close to waking him.

Of course, he's nowhere near sleep.

"No," he admits, rolling over to face the other bed in the room. His eyes have adjusted to the darkness enough that he can just barely make out Mikey's face in the light seeping around the edges of the curtain.

"Me either," Mikey whispers.

Tolya rolls his eyes. "No shit, Sherlock."

Mikey makes a rude noise. "I don't know why it's weird. We stayed in hotels all the time before."

"Yeah." Tolya agrees. "Sometimes I think I've spent more time sleeping in hotels than in a house."

"Makes sense." Mikey takes a breath. "But it's weird, right?"

Tolya nods, trusting Mikey to see it, or to correctly interpret the rustling noise. "Yeah."

"I spent so much time thinking about this," Mikey says. "Like, ever since I was a little kid. But now I'm here, and I can't fucking sleep."

"It's gonna be fine," Tolya says, his own anxiety slipping away now that he has someone else to talk through it. "We're probably only gonna get like a couple of shifts to play—"

Mikey sighs gustily. "I know, just—can you talk to me about something else. Something not like, boring, I don't know—"

"I've got you," Tolya says. "So you know about my dad, and how he played, but not a lot of people know that his mom, my babushka, lived with us for a lot of the time when I *was growing up. My mom had a rough recovery after I was born, and by the time she was better, well, they were all used to her being there. Anyway, she loved to cook, and she taught me how. Her favorite thing…"*

He keeps talking, keeping his voice even, doing his best to make Russian cooking as boring as he knows how to, until he hears the first soft snore coming from the other bed. Even though he expects to be awake longer, he finds himself slipping away, his breathing falling into rhythm with Mikey's.

6

———

MIKEY

M ikey wakes up, for once, without his head feeling like someone's hammering on it. He kind of wants to leap out of bed in celebration, broken arm or no broken arm, but when he sits up, his neck and shoulder muscles are so tight it hurts all the way down his spine.

"Fuck," he groans, wishing there was something handy to throw or kick. Except that would probably hurt. Being injured is for the fucking birds.

And then, of course, there's a knock on his bedroom door, because Tolly is an overprotective mother hen asshole. "You okay? Can I come in?"

"Yeah, come on," Mikey grumbles, getting cautiously to his feet. At least the vertigo is definitely gone. That's something.

The door opens and Tolly pokes his head in cautiously. "What's up? I heard something; wasn't sure—"

"I'm fine," Mikey says. He regrets his bitchy tone as soon as it comes out of his mouth, but honestly. He's on long-term IR, he's got a broken arm and a sort-of broken head, and he hasn't even had coffee. He's allowed to be a little snippy. "Honestly, I'm doing better. My head doesn't even hurt. But my neck and shoulders are so fucking tight, I almost can't tell."

"Bro, that sucks." Tolly's eyebrows pinch together like they always do when he's trying to come up with a solution. "Maybe you need to come with me to the arena, get the trainers to give you a massage? Or we could call some other place, but—"

Mikey nods. "But they probably don't know how to deal with a concussion. That's a good idea, though. If you don't mind playing chauffeur."

"Everybody'll be super stoked to see you, if you think you're up for it." Tolly looks like maybe he's regretting the suggestion a little. "But it's gonna be really loud, and bright."

"Yeah," Mikey agrees. As much as he hates it, Tolly's right, and there won't really be a good place for him to retreat to if it gets too much. Not without keeping the rest of the team from using it when they need it.

Tolly makes a considering noise. "Tell you what. We can turn on the main lights in here, open the curtains, see how you handle that?"

"Okay," Mikey says, because of course Tolly has a solution.

"Gimme a sec."

Tolly disappears from his doorway, probably to go make the living area as bright as possible. After a moment's thought, Mikey decides waiting to put on a shirt until he knows if he's going anywhere is the better option. But he does manage to maneuver into a pair of basketball shorts without falling over, so that counts as a victory, right?

"Okay, come on," Tolly says, pushing the door open wide. "You ready?"

"I guess," Mikey says, wincing as he gets to his feet. He can already imagine the stabbing pain in his head from the increased light levels, but hell, he already hurts. He'll risk a lot more if it means someone will work the tension out of his neck and shoulders, especially if he gets to soak in the massive hot tub in the trainers room after.

His instinct as he approaches the door is to squint, but that just sends another shooting pain down the sides of his neck. So he blinks slowly instead, hesitating for a long, long moment , dull red light filtering through his eyelids before he opens them again.

It's weird, seeing their apartment in full light instead of the dimness he's gotten used to since his injury. All the lights are on, morning sun streaming through the windows on two walls. Mikey keeps waiting for the pain to hit, but aside from some rapid blinking to let his eyes adjust, he's fine. "I'm fine."

"Sweet," Tolly says, squeezing his good shoulder

gently. "Let's get some clothes on you so we can head out after breakfast."

Mikey wants to argue, but it's November in Alberta. He can't just go out in basketball shorts and a coat, as tempting as that is. "Yeah, okay."

Even the prospect of having to be helped into his clothes like a child can't dampen his excitement. He feels like he can take a breath for the first time since he woke up in the hospital. And, judging from the way Tolly returns his grin, he's not the only one.

"Hey, dude," he blurts out, stopping Tolly with a hand on his arm. "Seriously, thanks for everything you've been doing. I would've lost my fucking mind a long time ago without you."

"Anytime," Tolly says, his eyes steady even as his cheeks go faintly pink. "I've got your back."

Mikey nods. "Yeah, I know. Just—thanks."

They stand there just grinning at each other for a few seconds longer before Tolly claps him on the shoulder again. "Come on, move your ass or you're gonna make me late."

"Fine, fine," Mikey sighs, but he can't stop smiling. It's gonna be a great day.

"READY TO GO?" Tolly asks as he comes into the trainer's room.

"Awww, do I have to?"

Mikey winces when he hears the whine in his voice, but seriously, he feels so fucking good right now. Sara the massage therapist—not to be confused with Sarah in PR, although both are terrifyingly good at their jobs and could probably kill a man without breaking a sweat—worked over his neck and shoulders, with his entire back added in for good measure. Then she'd shooed him into the hot tub and left him alone for a long, blissful soak. He might have napped—he's not sure.

"C'mon," Tolly coaxes. "Aren't you hungry? I thought we could hit up Niji on the way home."

Even without the sudden grumble of his stomach at the mention of food, Mikey would already have been half-out of the tub. Tolly's not a bad cook, and they have the meal service delivering them food, plus whatever restaurants deliver to their building. He's not starving to death or anything, but suddenly sushi sounds like the best idea anyone's ever had. "Well, what are you waiting for? Come help me get dressed!"

"What's the magic word?" Tolly laughs, but he's already grabbing a towel off the nearby stack, wrapping it around Mikey's shoulders as he climbs out of the tub.

"Pretty please?" Mikey asks, doing his best to channel Diana when she's trying to convince Dad to buy her something.

Except it suddenly feels weird to be doing that right now. With Tolly standing so close, his hands warm and sure as he dries Mikey off, the towel moving lower and lower. It's one of those moments where it seems weird that they're almost exactly the same height, when he notices dumb things like how Tolly's eyes aren't really blue, not all the way through, with the green and gold flecks around his pupil.

"Mikey?"

"Huh?"

From Tolly's tone, he's been trying to get his attention for awhile. He doesn't seem mad, though, so maybe he didn't have to repeat himself too many times. "Where are your clothes?"

"Oh, uh, Sara put them over there," he says, waving in the direction of the neat stack of clothes on the nearest chair.

It should be routine by now to have Tolly help him into his clothes, but Mikey keeps getting distracted by dumb things like the softness of Tolly's sweats when they brush against his bare legs, the way his hair flops into his eyes and he keeps raking it back, the way his eyes crinkle just a little at the corners when he smiles.

Finally, though, he's dressed again, and almost before Mikey knows it, they're settled in a booth at Niji, ordering their usual ridiculous assortment of sushi rolls. They don't even have to wait too long for the food to arrive, since they got there a little before the normal lunch rush. Everything is awesome—until he tries to open his chopsticks.

"Here," Tolly says quietly, taking them out of his hand and snapping them apart before handing them back.

Mikey takes a deep breath, doing his best to visualize what he's about to do. The chopsticks feel weird and clumsy in his left hand—not that he's any kind of expert with his right, but he can usually manage not to embarrass himself or drop half his meal all over his shirt.

"Bro, just use your fingers," Tolly says, setting down his own chopsticks and picking up a piece of sushi with his hands, dipping it in the sauce and popping it in his mouth.

Reluctantly, Mikey follows suit. It feels like admitting defeat, but it's all too easy to imagine the disaster that would ensue if he doesn't, the way his sushi would disintegrate all over the table and all over him. "Fine."

Except, thanks to his extreme lack of dexterity with his left hand, the piece of sushi falls apart just before it touches his lips. "Sh—ugar," Mikey hisses, just barely able to redirect the curse when he sees the curious eyes of the toddler in the next booth.

"Seriously?" Tolly asks, looking at him incredulously.

"I'm terrible with my left hand," Mikey says miserably. When he holds it up by way of illustration, the traces of rice, fish, and other filling smeared over it just make it sadder. "Unless I'm using it as a f—reaking shovel, this is probably just gonna keep happening."

Tolly shakes his head. "No wonder you end up wearing half your food. Why didn't you say something, bro? I'll ask the waitress for a fork next time she comes by."

They both look up, but the room has filled with people and their waitress is nowhere to be seen. "It's fine," Mikey says, doing his best to ignore the growling noise from his stomach before he can even finish speaking."

"I've got your back," Tolly says, picking up a piece of dragon roll, dipping it before holding it out to him.

Mikey eats it instinctively, only realizing when his mouth closes over Tolly's fingers how weirdly intimate this situation is. There's no going back now, though, and he's not about to spit out one of the best things he's ever eaten. He chews and swallows, doing his best to pretend that his face isn't heating, that he isn't replaying the graze of Tolly's thumb against his lower lip.

"Oh, excuse me," Tolly says, flagging down a waitress, thank fuck. "Can we get a fork? My friend here is kinda useless with his left hand."

Her eyes widen when she looks at Mikey. He gives a little wave with his casted hand by way of emphasis. "Oh, of course," she says, pulling a bundle of silverware rolled in a napkin out of her little apron. "I'm so sorry. Can I get you anything else?"

"No thanks," Mikey says, waiting as Tolly unrolls the napkin and taking the fork from him.

"Just let me know," she says, smiling down at Tolly in a way that Mikey's more used to seeing when they go out to clubs or bars. "My name's Alyssa."

Tolly returns her smile maybe a little too warmly. "Thanks so much."

With the fork, Mikey's actually able to maneuver a piece of sushi to his mouth by himself. That's a good thing, he tells himself sternly. He's an adult, and he should be able to feed himself. And there's no reason he should feel annoyed that Tolly's smiling at a pretty waitress, even if there's no way the waitress could know for sure that they aren't together. Well, like, obviously they're at the restaurant together, but still. They could totally be like, together together.

Mikey shakes his head, pulling that train of thought to a halt. Clearly hunger is making him delusional. He needs to focus on getting food in his mouth instead of on his shirt.

He manages to make it through lunch with no more mishaps, even if he doesn't talk much. Tolly doesn't either, though; they're both usually too busy shoving enough calories into their faces to worry about making conversation.

By the time the plates are empty of everything except some lonely ginger and wasabi, Mikey feels like he just played back-to-back games on the same day, completely wiped out. He slumps back against the booth, twirling his fork absently between his fingers and thumb.

"Hey, stay with me, okay?" Tolly says.

Mikey blinks his eyes open, not sure when he closed them. "Sorry dude, I'm just wiped."

"You're still recovering," Tolly says. "I'm just waiting for her to bring my card back and then we can get you home."

Nodding, Mikey does his best to keep his eyes open. It's not much longer before the waitress brings the little fake-leather folder with Tolly's credit card back. Mikey's sleepy, but not so sleepy that he doesn't notice the way she smiles at Tolly, or how she makes sure to let their fingers brush together when she hands him the folder.

"Come back and see me soon," she says, completely ignoring Mikey to give Tolly one last smile as she turns away.

Tolly doesn't seem to notice, opening the folder and taking out the slip and the pen to sign it. It's hard to tell for sure when it's upside down but—

"Dude, did she give you her number?" Mikey's question comes out a lot more accusatory than he'd meant it to, but seriously. He was right here the whole time. Rude.

"I guess," Tolly says, pushing the piece of paper with the phone number to the side and filling in the tip on the other one, his tongue poking out the corner of his mouth as he attempts to do the math.

Mikey sighs. "It doesn't have to be a perfectly even number. She'll be fine with whatever tip you give her."

He doesn't realize the possible dirty implications of the statement until Tolly looks at him with raised eyebrows. "Oh really? Just the tip?"

"Shut up," Mikey says, rolling his eyes but unable to hold back a laugh. "I'm a little annoyed, though. What if we were together? That would be super rude, hitting on you in front of me."

"Do you want to argue about this or do you want to go home and have a nap?" Tolly asks, completely ignoring Mikey's reasonable complaint. If only he didn't have a point.

Mikey sits up and starts sliding out of the booth. "Nap, definitely."

Getting out of the restaurant and into Tolly's car takes the last of his energy; he's pretty sure he falls asleep before they leave the parking lot.

WHEN MIKEY WAKES up in his own bed, afternoon light soft around the edges of the curtains, he only has the vaguest memory of Tolly guiding him into the apartment, taking off his shoes before letting him sprawl across the bed.

He feels drowsy, sluggish, like he could easily roll over and sleep for another several hours, but if he does that he's going to be wide awake at 3 am. So he forces himself to sit up, wincing at the soreness that returned to his neck and shoulders. It's not as bad as it was this morning, but Sara had to dig into his muscles pretty hard to get them to loosen up.

Still, it's nice to be able to move without bracing for vertigo, or nausea, or the stabbing pain in his head. He shuffles into his bathroom to piss, managing to aim well enough with his left hand to avoid making a mess. Washing his hands, as always, is awkward, but he manages, then wanders out to the living area, scratching idly at his stomach.

"Hey," Tolly says, looking up from the couch, controller in hand. "Good nap?"

"Yeah." Mikey sinks down on the couch next to him, yawning. "But now that they're cold, my neck and shoulders are a little sore again."

Tolly nods. "Sara doesn't play. Hang on, I have an idea."

"Okay," Mikey agrees. He's still not fully awake; sitting sounds like a good idea.

He watches idly as Tolly gets to a save point in his game—Dragon Blood or something, one of the fantasy RPGs he likes—and disappears into his bedroom. The background music from the game is kind of soothing, and Mikey's seriously considering just swinging his legs up on the couch for nap part two by the time Tolly reappears.

"C'mon," he says, offering a hand to pull Mikey up from the couch.

Still at least half-asleep, Mikey follows Tolya obediently through his unnaturally neat bedroom and into his bathroom. He stops dead just inside the door, blinking in surprise as he looks around, taking in the still-filling bathtub, the flickering light of candles and the scents filling the air, kind of like cologne but nicer. "Wow."

"It's no big deal," Tolly says, running his hand through his hair like he's embarrassed. "It's not the hot tub, but I thought it might help. Easier to keep your cast dry than in the shower. And the lights are super bright, and my mom bought these candles I never used—" he trails off like he has no idea where he was going with that, and honestly, neither does Mikey.

"Well, what are we waiting for?" Mikey says, pulling the hem of his t-shirt up as best he can.

As usual, Tolly steps in to help, like it's become automatic. With his assistance, it's only a few minutes until Mikey is stepping into the gloriously hot water, sitting back with a sigh.

It's a little tricky to keep his arm out of the water—even with two coatings of plastic wrap and a bag taped over the top, he's still worried about getting it wet. But if he tips to the side just slightly, most of his sore muscles should be under the water once the tub fills.

"I live here now," Mikey announces, opening his eyes just in time to see Tolly holding out a weird, brightly colored little ball. "What's that?"

"Bath bomb?" Tolly says. "It smelled nice, and the lady at the store said it's one of the best ones for relaxing."

Mikey has only the vaguest idea of what a bath bomb is; he's heard Andrea and Diana talking about them, but mostly just comparing different ones. He's not usually a bath guy, since showers are faster and more efficient, but apparently that's changing. "Sure, why the fuck not?"

Tolly drops the little ball in the water and it starts immediately spinning and foaming around like crazy, leaving trails of color in the water when it moves, filling the room with the smell of peppermint.

"Wow," Mikey says, watching it move. "Dude, is that glitter?"

"The lady didn't say anything about glitter," Tolly says, leaning down to look more closely at the water.

Mikey pokes at the water. "Well, that's definitely glitter. It looks like stars."

Ducking his head, Tolly mutters something to quiet to hear under the sound of water rushing into the tub, echoing off the hard surfaces of the bathroom

"What? I can't hear you," Mikey says, half because he's genuinely curious and half to poke at Tolly.

"It's called Intergalactic," Tolly says, his face resigned.

Mikey laughs, harder than he has in weeks. "You giant nerd. I bet that's the whole reason you bought it, because it reminded you of Star Trek."

"I thought it smelled nice!" Tolly protests. A pause. "And it reminded me of Star Trek."

"It does smell nice," Mikey agrees. The peppermint smell is crisp and relaxing, and in combination with the hot water and the dim light, he can practically feel the tension leaving his muscles.

Tolly leans over to turn off the water when it starts sloshing into that little thing that keeps it from overflowing. "I guess I'll get out of here, leave you to it."

"Or—"

"Or?" he says, turning back with his eyebrows raised.

Mikey puts on his best Puss-in-Boots eyes. "Or you could grab the book and read to me while I'm in the bath."

"By candlelight?" Tolly asks, not lowering his eyebrows.

"Don't front, I know you have that dorky little book light you take on roadies," Mikey says, then remembers he's supposed to be asking for something, not chirping. "C'mon, please? Look, the water's all colored, you can't even see my dick. Not that you haven't seen my dick before. I mean--"

Tolly sighs, but the corners of his mouth are tipping up like he's trying not to smile. "Fine, I'll be right back."

"Yes!" Mikey fist-pumps with his good hand. "You're the best."

"Yeah, yeah," Tolly says, leaving the room, but Mikey can tell he's smiling.

Day after moving in

"I cannot look at these boxes any longer," Mikey declares, flopping down onto the couch. "And I'm starving."

"Pizza?" Tolly asks, looking up from where he sits cross-legged on the floor, organizing his DVDs onto the entertainment center. Seriously, who even has DVDs anymore?

Mikey rolls his eyes. "I'm pretty sure the nutritionist would hunt us down like animals if we had pizza two days in a row. Something with protein and a decent carb load."

"There's that pasta place close to the arena—"

"Which we had the day before yesterday," Mikey points out.

It's Tolly's turn to roll his eyes, which is rude. It's not Mikey's fault he's right. "Fine, then, you make a suggestion."

Like he thinks Mikey can't or won't. Mikey whips out his phone and hits up his friend Google.

"Sushi," he announces after scrolling through options. "It's time to find our next favorite restaurant."

"How are you always this excited?" Tolly asks, but he's getting to his feet, so Mikey wins.

He shrugs. "It's a gift. Come on, it's food time. Bet you five dollars I can get the waitress to think we're a couple."

"Why would you do that?" Tolly looks like he's already dreading the answer.

"Um, because I can? Besides, when people think you're a cute couple, sometimes you get free stuff. I'm a growing boy, Tolly!"

Tolly rolls his eyes again, deliberately bumping into Mikey on his way toward the door. "Whatever."

"You'll see," Mikey proclaims, following in his wake. "Just wait for it."

"I'll be fine," Mikey insists from where he stands in the doorway, watching Tolya pack. "I don't need a babysitter. Look, I'm standing upright and everything. No hands."

Tolya looks over to where he is, of course, waving his hands in the air by way of illustration. "Yeah, but what if you have a setback? And you can't call anyone to come help you? I'd feel better if you weren't alone."

"Dude." Mikey sighs dramatically. "I haven't been alone for more than an hour or two since I left the hospital.

"So you haven't been sleeping alone?" Tolya asks. He probably shouldn't, but it's right there. And it feels good to be able to poke at Mikey in something like their normal relationship.

He barely manages to keep a straight face at the outrage in Mikey's expression. "You know what I mean," Mikey practically growls. "That's not the point."

"What is the point then, Kevin?" Tolya asks, leaning on the name because he can't seem to resist needling Mikey right now, despite his best efforts.

Mikey closes his eyes and visibly takes a breath. "The point," he grits out, not sounding remarkably calmer, "Is that I can survive for twenty hours until you get back from New Mexico, especially since I'll be sleeping for at least eight of them."

Tolya wants to argue more, wants to put his foot down and say that he's calling the home health aides again and that's final. But looking at the stubborn set of Mikey's jaw, he knows it's a losing battle that he doesn't have the time and energy to win. "Fine," he sighs.

The grin that spreads across Mikey's face is almost blindingly bright. Despite his reservations and worries, Tolya can't help smiling back.

"It's gonna be fine," Mikey says, turning to leave the doorway. "You'll see."

"I hope so," Tolya mutters.

By the time he gets in his car to drive home from the airport, Tolya is a ball of nerves. He hadn't realized how much he'd counted on getting those regular updates from the aide until he was faced with radio silence. His imagination keeps painting pictures of Mikey passed out on the floor, unable to call for help.

He has no idea how fast he was driving to get home and honestly no memory of most of the drive, his brain too busy coming up with possible nightmare scenarios. Pushing his door open with one hand while putting the car in park with the other, he grabs his bag and heads off for their apartment at what would be a run for most people.

The elevator ride up to their floor seems to take even longer than the drive, every second crawling by until he's about to jump out of his skin, practically running down the hall to their door. When he tries to get his key into the lock, he realizes his hands are shaking. It feels like it takes forever to get the door unlocked, but it's probably actually only a few seconds. Dread twists in the pit of his stomach at the darkness of the apartment when he turns the knob and shoulders the door open.

"Mikey?" he calls softly. Maybe Mikey's just asleep, and that's why everything is dark.

The low groan coming from the couch tells him otherwise. Somehow, Tolya manages to drop his bag, close the door, and cross the room without tripping and falling on his face, although it's close a couple of times. Mikey is stretched out on the couch, he sees when he gets closer, his eyes adjusting to the dim room, wearing nothing but a pair of boxers, arm flung over his face.

"Hey," he says softly, squatting down next to the couch. "What's going on?"

"Headache," Mikey mumbles, not moving his good arm off of his eyes. "Hurts."

Tolya lets out a quick breath of relief. "Did you take anything?"

"Nuh-uh," Mikey says.

"Okay," Tolya says, letting out the breath he didn't know he was holding. Of course he didn't take anything. Although from the looks of things, it probably hurts to even think about moving. "I'm gonna get you something. I'll be right back."

Thankfully the Tylenol and ibuprofen are still where they left them on the dining table, so it only takes him a second to grab them. He detours to the fridge for a Gatorade in case Mikey's dehydrated—who knows how long he's been lying there on the couch—and books it back to the living area as fast as he can without making a lot of noise.

"Here," he breathes as quietly as possible, shaking out a couple of pills and putting them in Mikey's hand.

It takes a little bit of coaxing, but finally Mikey gets the meds in his mouth, lets Tolya coax him to a sitting position so he can wash them down with Gatorade.

"When was the last time you ate or drank anything?" Tolya asks, lifting the Gatorade back to Mikey's mouth for him to take another sip.

"About ten seconds ago," Mikey snarks, which has to be a good sign. "Are you gonna feed me the whole fucking bottle like I'm a baby?"

Tolya rolls his eyes. "Only if you keep whining about

it. What about before, smart guy? Did you eat anything today?"

"I had breakfast," Mikey mutters, taking another sip. "I was about to get lunch when this hit."

After a few quick calculations, Tolya pulls his phone out. "I'm ordering delivery. Are you nauseated?"

Mikey starts to shake his head, then winces. "No, just the head."

"Okay, I'm getting pizza," Tolya says, deciding to err on the side of getting food into Mikey's stomach for the first time in probably eight hours rather than worrying about his nutrition plan. After all, it's not like he's playing anytime soon.

By the time the pizza arrives, the meds seem to have taken effect; Mikey still winces a little when he moves too fast, but he wolfs down half of the pizza and the salad without any problems, settling back on the couch and eyeing Tolya's beer jealously.

"Do I get to say 'I told you so' now?" Tolya asks.

"Aww, dude, c'mon," Mikey says, rolling his eyes. "I didn't like, fall and die in a puddle of my own vomit. I had a headache. I was fine."

Tolya sighs, taking another sip. "Yeah, but you might not have been fine."

"I'm just—" Mikey trails off in a huff. After a minute of gathering his thoughts, he tries again. "I can't fucking do anything. I can't cook—"

"You couldn't cook before either," Tolya interjects, just to see if it makes him laugh.

Sure enough, Mikey thumps him with one of the throw pillows Tolya's mom sent along when he first moved out. "Fuck you. I can't fucking feed myself without spilling food all over myself unless it's something like pizza. I can't take a shower without you hovering in the hallway to see if I fall down and crack my head open. I can't even jerk off anymore."

The words hang there in the air between them, Mikey's cheeks turning a dull red as he realizes what he just said.

"Really?" Tolya can't help but ask.

Mikey huffs. "Dude, you saw how terrible I am with my left hand. I can't even eat sushi without getting it everywhere. I mean, I can, but it doesn't—I don't—"

He'd like to blame it on the beer, but he knows better. The words that come out of his mouth next are a hundred percent him, even if he has apparently lost his damn mind at some recent point in time. "I could give you a hand with that," Tolya says. "If you want."

For a couple of seconds they sit there, frozen. Like Schroedinger's cat, there's no way to know what's going to happen next until It does. Tolya can see Mikey gaping at him out of the corner of his eye, feel his own face heating. But he doesn't take it back.

"Really?" Mikey says finally. "Because seriously, that's above and beyond—"

Tolya shrugs. "Like I said, if you want. If not, no harm, no foul."

"And if I do?" Mikey asks quietly. "What happens then?"

"Then I ask where you wanna do this," Tolya answers, just as quietly. "Here? Well, maybe not here. I don't wanna have to clean jizz off the couch. Your bed?"

Mikey blinks at him for a second before shaking off his confusion. "Uh, yeah."

Getting to his feet, Tolya holds a hand out to Mikey, who takes it after only a short hesitation. Normally he'd let go of it once he pulled Mikey to his feet—but nothing about this situation is normal. It's terrifying, but also freeing. There's nothing to stop Tolya from lacing their fingers together as he leads the way to Mikey's bedroom.

It gets a little awkward then, when they're in Mikey's space. This isn't—they're blurring the lines, Tolya thinks, his mind spinning a mile a minute. Not that there were a lot of lines between him and Mikey to begin with, even before his injury. And what with the showering together and the helping him dress and the feeding him—okay, maybe he's over-thinking this.

"Lube?" he asks, even though he's pretty sure—yeah, Mikey pulls open the top drawer of his bedside table and takes out a bottle of lube. He gets a quick glimpse of some kind of sex toy—it's bright purple and glittery, which is unexpected—before Mikey pushes the drawer closed again, his cheeks flushing even redder.

"You don't have—" Mikey starts, because seriously, he's the stubbornest, idiot ever.

Tolya hooks his thumbs in the waistband of Mikey's boxers and tugs him closer, smiling a little smugly when that shuts him up. "I know I don't have to, dumbass. Have I ever offered to do something I'm not okay with?"

Mikey swallows, his eyes huge and dark up close like this, his tongue darting out to wet his lips. "No," he says, his voice low and rough.

"Can I kiss you?" Tolya asks. He second-guesses the words as soon as they're out of his mouth, but hell. It's already weird. Might as well go for broke, make it good for Mikey. "Unless—"

"Yeah," Mikey breathes.

Tolya gets one hand around the back of Mikey's neck, pulling him in until their lips meet. It's soft at first, both of them tentative, but then Mikey makes a noise, his teeth scraping lightly over Tolya's lower lip. He licks inside when Tolya's lips part, hot and wet and good, his hands cradling Tolya's face and tilting it just so.

At some point Tolya's other hand ended up on Mikey's ass, pressing them together from chest to hip. Mikey's cock is a hard line next to his, separated only by a few layers of fabric, pressure almost exactly where he wants it. He has no idea which of them starts moving first, barely knows where he ends and Mikey begins, just that there's a slow, delicious friction.

He's breathing hard when they separate; it takes a moment for him to remember that he's supposed to be helping Mikey out here, not dry-humping him. "Hey," he says, startled by the rasp in his voice. "C'mon, let's get these off, get you on the bed."

Mikey makes a protesting noise, but lets go with one

last tantalizing brush of fingers across the back of Tolya's neck. Getting his boxers off is a matter of seconds, pulling the elastic waist down over his ass and letting them fall to the floor. Tolya urges Mikey down onto the bed, then has to go back to search for the lube, dropped heedlessly on the floor.

When he turns back to the bed, his breath catches in his throat. Mikey looks like porn, sprawled naked across the sheets, left hand stroking lazily over his hard cock as he watches Tolya.

"I thought you couldn't jerk off," Tolya says, climbing onto the mattress and straddling Mikey's legs with only a second's hesitation.

"I mean, I can do it, obviously." Mikey shrugs. "But I can't get there. It's frustrating as fuck."

Flipping the lube open, Tolya squeezes some out into his palm and sets the bottle aside. "Well, let's see if we can fix that."

"Wait," Mikey blurts, biting his lip. "Can you —never mind."

"What?" Tolya asks. From a purely practical standpoint, this is going to work better if Mikey tells him what does it for him. But also, he just wants to know. "C'mon, you can ask. If I don't want to, I'll say no."

Mikey nods, taking a deep breath. "Can you take off your shirt? I feel weird, being naked while you're dressed."

"You feel weird?" Tolya teases, trying to take his shirt off one-handed, or at least without smearing lube all over it. "Or you wanna look at my hot body while you get off?"

Instead of blushing, though, Mikey gives him a slow up and down that has even more heat prickling under his skin. "A little of both," he says, fucking up into his fist.

He doesn't protest when Tolya reaches out, replacing the hand on his cock with his own lube-slick one. "Okay," Tolya says, tightening his hand experimentally as he strokes, watching Mikey's face and body for clues. "Gonna tell me what you want?"

"Fuck," Mikey groans. The flush on his cheeks has spread down his throat and across the top of his chest. "A little faster?"

Tolya obliges him, adding a twist of his hand over the head that always feels good when he does it to himself. Apparently it translates, because Mikey makes a soft noise, his hips jerking up off the bed.

"Yeah, Tolly, like that," Mikey breathes, his eyes fluttering closed.

He's never thought anything of Mikey using his team nickname, but it feels weird here, like this. "Tolya," he corrects, his own voice gone breathy and soft.

Mikey's eyes open again at that, searching his face. "Tolya," he says slowly, reaching up to curl a hand around Tolya's free arm. "Feels good. I'm close."

"Good," Tolya says, doing his best to ignore the shiver that runs through his body at Mikey's words. This isn't about him. "What do you need?"

"Just this," Mikey breathes. His hips roll, thrusting up into Tolya's hand, the expression on his face somewhere between pained and ecstatic. "Oh, fuck. Yeah, just—yeah—"

Tolya focuses on keeping the same pace and rhythm, speeding up his strokes a little when Mikey starts fucking into his hand in earnest, wordlessly begging for more. "Come on," he murmurs, not even thinking about the words coming out of his mouth. "Come on, Misha—"

Mikey comes with a sharp intake of breath, thrusting raggedly, striping his stomach and chest with the force of it. Tolya keeps stroking until he's squirming and shuddering with oversensitivity, pulling his hand carefully away.

"I'll be right back, okay?" he says, looking down at the mess of lube and semen on his hand. He could wipe it on the sheets, but that seems rude. And if he stays in here, with Mikey sprawled all loose and sated across the sheets, he might do something stupid. Stupider. The stupid ship has clearly sailed.

"'Kay," Mikey murmurs, his eyes still closed as Tolya escapes to the ensuite, his hard cock bobbing comically in midair.

Washing his hands doesn't take enough time for the stupid organ to calm down, sadly, and neither does wetting a warm washcloth. Fortunately, Mikey's eyes are still closed when he returns, although they fly open when Tolya starts to clean the mess off his chest and stomach.

"You—I can—"

Tolya bats his hand away when he reaches for the cloth. "I've got it."

Apparently Mikey's less stubborn post-orgasm—Tolya tucks that little tidbit away for future reference, then kicks himself for assuming this is going to happen again. He makes quick work of cleaning up, tossing the cloth in the clothes hamper in the corner.

"I'm gonna get you a water and a Gatorade," he announces, disappearing to the kitchen.

The cold air of the fridge doesn't help with his erection either, but it gives him time to take a deep breath before returning to Mikey's room. And some deity must be smiling on him, because Mikey's asleep already, snoring softly, when he pushes the door open.

Tolya sets the bottles on his bedside table and turns off the light, closing the door carefully behind him and retreating to his own room. And if it only takes a few strokes over his cock before he's coming too, shaking with the force of it, well. Nobody else has to know.

Sometime in October

"Shit," Tolya says softly, letting go of his cock like it had burned him. Well, figuratively it kind of did, he thinks with a humorless chuckle. Certainly having the image of Mikey pop into his head when jerking off was just as startling.

It's not like he's never pictured a friend while jerking off before, or a teammate. Brains are weird, shit happens, and he can usually just go with it, brush it off after he's gotten his rocks off. But for some reason his brain is doing the equivalent of the Kill Bill sirens.

Maybe it's because Mikey's his d-partner. Jerking off to his d-partner has got to be a bad idea. Especially since his d-partner is also his roommate, who's rapidly becoming his best friend. If he starts fantasizing about Mikey too, who knows what kind of dumb ideas might start rattling around in there. Better to just cut the whole thing off now.

Determined to start off right, he turns to his computer to pull up some helpful porn. And if his mind keeps drifting in directions it shouldn't before he forcibly cuts it off, well, he needs practice.

Nobody else has to know.

8

Mikey wakes up feeling better than he has in weeks, loose and relaxed. Even the sunlight glowing around the edges of the blackout curtains doesn't bother him; he kind of wants to pull them aside and bask in the light like a cat.

His brain finally comes online enough to remember what happened last night, why he's lying here naked. It's a good memory—the hungry way Tolly kissed him, the warm, sure strokes of his hand—but Mikey can't enjoy it as much as he'd like without guilt creeping in. Sure, he's injured, which is how the whole situation with Tolly—Tolya—giving him a hand came to be.

But Mikey's always prided himself on being the kind of person who reciprocates; equal opportunity orgasms for all. And what did he do last night? Passed out like a teenager who's never had an orgasm in company before, like the worst kind of dudebro stereotype, and left Tolya to take care of himself.

Not cool.

Riding a wave of guilt and determination, Mikey swings himself out of his bed and makes his way to the bathroom. He's going to deal with this—as soon as he takes care of some more pressing business.

He can't help but enjoy the fact that he's moving around mostly without pain. Sure, his right arm aches and itches under the cast, but his head is clear and his muscles are warm and relaxed. It's a state of well-being he was worried he'd never get back to for awhile, torturing himself with stories he's heard about guys who never recovered from concussions.

Every day he wakes up without his head hurting feels like a gift, something he would've taken for granted even a few months ago. But today, with his head clear and the possibility of doing something about his morning wood other than ignoring it, he's feeling pretty damn good. Even the exercise of getting into a pair of boxers one-handed, after considering and rejecting the direct approach of just showing up naked, doesn't dampen his spirits.

He doesn't run out of steam until he finds himself hesitating outside of Tolya's door, feeling unaccountably shy. Which is dumb, he tells himself fiercely. They've been living in each others pockets since they got this apartment months ago. Plus Tolya spent last night taking care of him, and then literally jerking him off. He's seen everything of Mikey there is to see.

That truth is both scary and strangely freeing.

Taking a deep breath, he lifts his hand and knocks lightly on the door, hopefully lightly enough that Tolya can ignore it if he's not awake yet.

"Come in," Tolya calls from inside, his voice thick with sleep.

"Morning," Mikey says, pushing the door open and sticking his head inside. "You awake? I can come back later."

Tolya shakes his head, squinting a little against the light coming through the open door. "Nah, I was gonna get up in a minute. Did you need something?"

Mikey can't ask for a better opening than that. "I just wanted to say thanks for, you know. Last night. And I want to get you back next time."

"I—you—" He can practically see the thoughts crossing Tolya's face, written there as clearly as the books he can't read right now. "It's okay, you know. I mean—"

"Unless you don't want a next time," he hastens to add. "But like, sorry I passed out on you so fast. Seriously, though, I know I can't use my hand, but my mouth works just fine."

Tolya blinks rapidly at him. "I, uh. Yeah. I mean, if you want."

"Yeah, I want." Mikey closes the door behind him, crossing to Tolya's bed. He hesitates by the side of it; he kind of wants to just climb up, but— "Maybe it'll work better, with the arm, if you swing your legs over the side of the bed?"

"Oh, yeah, sorry," Tolya says, scrambling to push the covers back. He's naked underneath, his cock hard already, the foreskin pulled back under the head. "This okay?"

Mikey lowers himself to his knees between Tolya's legs, good hand braced on his thigh. "Yeah. How about you? This okay? I mean, we don't have to—"

Tolya laughs a little, wrapping a hand around the base of his cock where it's bobbing in midair, inches from Mikey's face. "I think it's pretty obvious how okay with this I am."

"Yeah, but, like, consent," Mikey says, licking his lips. "I don't wanna pressure you into this if you don't want to."

"Misha," Tolya says, bringing his free hand up to frame Mikey's face. "I would really enjoy a blow job."

Excellent, consent established. Good to go. But— "Wait a minute. You called me that last night, too."

Tolya's face goes pink across his cheekbones and down his neck. "There isn't a nickname in Russian for Kevin, but—"

"It's okay," Mikey says, cutting off the embarrassed babble with a kiss to Tolya's hipbone. "I like it. You can call me Misha all you want."

It's kind of gratifying, how quickly Tolya goes quiet when Mikey's cheek brushes against his hand, his cock. Like maybe Mikey has a shot at actually reciprocating here, taking Tolya apart the way he took Mikey apart the night before.

With that in mind, he doesn't just dive in like he might otherwise. Turning his head, he presses an open-mouthed kiss to the shaft of Tolya's cock, right above where his hand is holding it, letting his tongue linger on the hot, thin skin.

Tolya inhales sharply, almost like he's surprised. It's encouraging, though, so Mikey does it again, a little higher, lets himself explore. He circles his tongue around the head, lingering on the sensitive spot just underneath until Tolya's thigh starts shaking under his hand.

"Misha, come on," Tolya breathes. He lifts one hand to Mikey's head, his fingertips just barely brushing Mikey's hair before he pulls them back, pressing his palm down on the bed.

"You can put your hand on my head," Mikey says, looking up at him. He gets a little distracted for a second by how wrecked Tolya looks already, his face and chest flushed, his lip bitten red. "Just don't like, push me down or anything, okay?"

Tolya's hand comes back up, hovering in the air before curling gently around the back of Mikey's skull. "This good?"

Mikey nods, turning his attention back to the task at hand. It's a good thing Tolya's holding his cock steady, since Mikey only has one good hand to work with. All he has to do is lean forward and close his mouth over the head, sliding slowly down until it hits the back of his throat and he has to come back up.

"Oh, fuck," Tolya groans, his hand flexing in Mikey's

hair. But he doesn't push. "God, fuck, I'm not gonna last, Misha—"

That's all the encouragement Mikey needs to start moving, up and down, letting his lips drag over the shaft with each movement. He swirls his tongue on the way up, nudges the tip of it under the foreskin on the way down, judging his success by the speed and fervency of Tolya's cursing above him.

He's doing his best to remember everything that ever felt good when he got a blowjob, but to be honest most of his memories just boil down to "hot wet good." So he explores and experiments, trying different things and doing his best to ignore his own erection because this is not about him.

It doesn't all work, but Mikey's always been very coachable. Within a gratifyingly short period of time, Tolya's hips are hitching up off the bed a little bit, trying to fuck up into his mouth.

"Misha," Tolya says, frantically, doing his best to pull Mikey's head up. "Misha, I'm going—I'm close —fuck—I—"

Mikey's had some embarrassing mishaps when he's tried to swallow in the past, but hell, Tolya's not going to make fun of him if he fucks it up. He moves faster, adds a little bit of suction at the top, every other trick that Tolya seems to like. Within a few seconds, Tolya goes still under him, flooding his mouth with his bitter-salty flavor.

Swallowing like it's his job, for once Mikey manages not to choke himself or make a mess everywhere. He maybe even overdoes it a little, swallowing over and over until Tolya makes a pained noise, pulling free of his lips.

Mikey sits back on his heels and drags the back of his hand over his mouth. His own cock is hard and straining against the fabric of his boxers, but he can't look away from Tolya's face, can't help but lean into Tolya's touch on his face.

"Fuck," Tolya says thickly, blinking his eyes open. His hands are clumsy as he pulls Mikey up, but Mikey goes willingly, stumbling to his feet and letting Tolya pull him in for a long, soft kiss.

Despite the arousal thrumming through his veins, the urgent drumbeat of his pulse, Mikey doesn't really want to rush the kiss. There's something about the way Tolya cradles his face in his hands, the way their lips cling together, parting and returning, that makes him want to savor everything about this moment.

Of course, nothing lasts forever. When he shifts closer, trying to get more skin contact, find more of Tolya to touch, his cock brushes against Tolya's stomach, reminding him forcibly that he's been hard for what feels like an eternity.

"Here," Tolya says, breaking the kiss. "Let me—"

Mikey feels his eyes roll back in his head as Tolya nudges his boxers down with one hand, circling the base of his cock with the other. "Oh, fuck," he groans. His good hand lands on Tolya's shoulder just in time, his legs going wobbling with Tolya's first gentle stroke.

"Okay, hang on."

He's not exactly proud of the whimpering noise he makes when Tolya lets go of his cock, but he figures there's probably a general amnesty on chirping people for noises made during sex. At least he sure hopes there is. "C'mon," he says, opening his eyes. "I'm so close, Tolya—"

"And if you fall down and crack your head again, do you want to explain what you were doing to the ER doctors? Or Coach? Or your mom?" Tolya asks with a little smirk, nudging him toward the bed. "C'mon, sit down before you fall down."

"Fine," Mikey says, allowing himself to be steered onto the bed.

At first he just goes to sit on the edge, but Tolya just shakes his head. "C'mon, lay down. Easier on my knee this way."

Once he's settled to Tolya's satisfaction, stretched out across the sheets, he feels a little self-conscious at first. Tolya's just looking at him. It's not like this is the first time someone's looked at him like this, like they kind of want to eat him alive. But having that person be Tolya is—it's weird, okay. He and Tolya are d-partners and roomies and friends, but not this. Not until now.

But then Tolya's hand closes around his cock, and all of that seems much, much less important. Before he can actually get back to formulating any thoughts other than "yes" and "more," Tolya bends over. As soon as his cock is engulfed in warm, wet heat, Mikey gives up hope of his brain working and just lets himself feel.

"God, fuck," he breathes. Everything is Tolya: Tolya's

mouth on his cock, Tolya's hands on his hips, Tolya's taste lingering on his tongue. He's surrounded by the smell of sex, the wet, obscene sounds. Looking down his body, seeing Tolya's mouth stretched wide around his cock, his lashes fluttering against his cheekbones, is so overwhelming that all he can do is stammer out a warning before coming a few seconds later.

Tolya pulls off after the first few seconds, replacing his mouth with his hand and stroking him through it until he's shuddering with oversensitivity. The mattress shifts under him as Tolya rolls to the side, sprawling across the other side, their legs barely brushing each other.

If it was any other time than the moments right after an orgasm, Mikey's pretty sure he'd be feeling awkward right now. But as time goes on, and his brain comes back online, it seems more and more natural that he doesn't, even though he keeps poking at the absence like a missing tooth, checking to see if it hurts.

Maybe it makes sense, though. This is Tolya, after all. From the first moment they met, they just clicked. Sunshine likes to joke about them being drift compatible, and maybe he's right. Mikey can't think of any other friend that he could exchange hand jobs and blow jobs with and have it not be awkward. But with Tolya, it works. They work.

"High five," he finally says, breaking the not-awkward silence and holding his good hand up.

Tolya eyes him narrowly. "Why are we high fiving?"

"Because we're fucking awesome at sex, duh," Mikey says.

"You're ridiculous," Tolya answers, but he has to know by now that Mikey's going to keep his hand up there as long as it takes. His high-five is reluctant, but it happens.

Mikey will take it.

First day of training camp

"Petrov! Michaelson!" The skills coach barks the names. "Let's see it."

Mikey skates up to his position, keeping the other guy—Petrov—in the corner of his vision. There's something familiar about that name, but he's too busy trying to focus on the passing drill they're about to run to remember what it is. Probably not that important, anyway.

The nice thing about going last is that he got to watch everyone else do it. The shitty thing about going last is that everyone gets to watch you, and you have no fucking excuse if you fuck it up.

At the sound of the whistle, his body bursts into motion, like it knows what to do without input from his brain. The puck comes zooming in from his left, like it's magnetized to his tape, and he one-times it to his left without thinking, almost without looking.

He's expecting it to go wide, but instead it comes back to him, and he sends it back again. And again, and again. It's almost like he can feel where Petrov is going to be without looking. They finish the drill, looping around behind the net at the other end of the ice.

Mikey holds his hand out without thinking as they come close, forgetting for a second that this isn't BU, that Petrov doesn't know him. But then Petrov bumps a fist into his, grinning widely under his helmet, and Mikey can't help grinning back.

"Fucking drift compatible, man!" someone yells from the cluster of players watching them.

Even the coach is smiling when they make it back to the other end. "Not bad," he says, nodding at both of them. "Not bad at all."

They get a bit of a reprieve while he explains the next drill, starts the next d-pair going. Mikey watches, but he's aware of Petrov still at his side, too. "I'm Mikey," he says under his breath.

"Tolly," Petrov replies.

It's lunch before they get another chance to talk, but that's okay. They're communicating in their own way, with passes and drills until Mikey's half-forgotten what it's like not to have Tolly on the ice with him. His worry about staying up for the season has mostly disappeared; he knows, even without the approving looks and words from the coaches, that he's playing some of the best hockey of his life. And this is just practice; just the first day of camp.

It's just going to get better from here.

9

TOLYA

Tolya skates off the ice at the end of practice, sweating, his body aching slightly with the bone-deep satisfaction of physical exertion, of having pushed himself to his limits. It still feels weird, playing with Lightning instead of Misha—instead of Mikey, he corrects himself. But it was a good practice, one of those where everything clicks. Even though he just spent the better part of an hour running drills, he feels invigorated, energized. Like he could drink some Gatorade and then go out and run a race or something.

Stripping off his practice jersey, he accepts a towel from the new equipment manager—Caitlin, he thinks. Sweat drips into his eyes as he wipes his face before starting to take his pads off.

He's untaping his socks when someone sits down next

to him. At first he doesn't think much of it; the locker room is full of guys. But then Sunshine asks "How're you doing? How's Mikey?"

Tolya's face goes hot at the memory of what he and Misha were doing this morning, but that's—that's not what Sunshine is asking. He's just checking on a teammate, being his usually friendly self.

"He's good," he says, thankful that the flush on his cheeks probably just looks like it's left over from practice, not because of anything embarrassing. "The headaches are pretty much gone. The doctor thinks he can start physical therapy soon, keep his strength up."

"Good, good," Sunshine says, taking off his chest guard, but he still looks worried. "And look, don't freak out about the rumors, okay?"

"The rumors," Tolya repeats, his mind spinning around in circles. Because seriously, what rumors?

Sunshine shakes his head. "They're not gonna trade him. We have plenty of guys, plenty of cap space. Hardly anyone else is injured. It's gonna be fine."

"Right," Tolya says numbly. Suddenly he feels like he's just been checked into the boards, all the air gone out of his lungs.

Thankfully, he doesn't have to keep making conversation. Sunshine finishes stripping down and heads into the showers, while Tolya takes off the rest of his gear on autopilot. He keeps fumbling the motions that should be automatic, his attention scattered around the room, his mind a spiral of worry and fear. It takes every bit of willpower he possesses not to pull his phone out right there. But someone will notice, someone will ask. If the rumors are as widespread as Sunshine thinks—Tolya would rather find that out in private.

It's not any better when he finally gets into the showers, sadly. The white noise of water hitting tile, the pounding heat against sore muscles usually relaxes him, but not today. Scrubbing down seems to take twice as long as usual, his hands clumsy with worry and distraction and the thought of losing Misha so soon.

It feels kind of like he's crawling through thick, sticky mud, the way every routine thing is taking forever to accomplish. The only real benefit is that, by the time he gets back out into the locker room to get dressed, almost everyone is gone. He can pull out his phone and tap on the little Google search bar, type in "Kevin Michaelson trade rumors."

Even though they upgraded the wifi last year, it still seems to take an eternity before the results load. Tolya would like to think this means that there isn't anything to find—but he knows better, even before the first headline pops up.

It's mostly blogs so far, nothing official, or even semi-official. People speculating, because that's what people do. He should be relieved, should put his phone in his pocket and get ready to head home for lunch and a nap.

Instead, he finds himself tapping on the first result, dropping down to sit on the bench as he starts reading. The more he reads, the worse he feels, but he can't help himself, like flexing a sore muscle to see if it still hurts. And oh, boy, does it hurt. This guy, whoever he is—Tolya scrolls to the top, checks the name—this girl, this Genevieve Armand, knows her stuff. She's pulling out comparisons of other teams who traded guys on long-term IR, or who sent them down.

By the time he finishes the blog post, Tolya feels mildly ill, although he's not sure if that's from hunger or anxiety. Either way, being here isn't going to help. He ties his shoes, shoulders his bag, and leaves, praying to whatever gods are listening that he doesn't meet anyone on the way out.

As he makes his way through the cavernous, deserted back corridors of the arena, the hollow feeling in his stomach solidifies into a craving for his grandmother's piroshki. He's too distracted to remember which of the ingredients they have at home, but there's a Safeway on the way home.

Hey, he texts his mother. *Want to make piroshki. Can you send me the recipe?*

Who are you and what have you done with my son? she sends back almost instantly. *We will pay whatever ransom you ask, just please send us our son back*

He rolls his eyes. *Ha ha, Mama. I'm just hungry.*

All right, she says, even though he can practically see the skeptical look he'd be getting if they were face-to-face. *I'll send it. Make extra for Kevin, okay? Help him recover faster.*

I will, he promises. *Love you*

I love you, too, mishka. Send me a picture when you're done, I'll show your babushka

The next text chime is a picture of the recipe card, slightly spattered with grease and flour and other substances—"never trust a neat cook, mishka," his grandmother always says. It's still legible, though, so he puts the phone in his pocket and starts his car. He can do this.

He can do this.

"DID you get mugged on the way home?" Misha asks as Tolya comes through the door, even though his arms loaded down with grocery bags. "By very specific muggers who give you groceries?"

"Sorry," Tolya apologizes, trying to ignore the amount of Misha's skin currently visible, since apparently basketball shorts are the sum total of his outfit today. "I should've texted, or called."

Misha shrugs bare shoulders, following him into the kitchen. "I'm still not supposed to use the phone, so it wouldn't have done any good, probably."

"Are you trying to tell me you wouldn't have answered it?" Tolya asks, raising his eyebrows.

There's no immediate answer, confirming his suspicions, although Misha at least has the good grace to look a little embarrassed. "Only if it was an emergency," he finally says.

"And how would you know if it was an emergency?

Actually, scratch that, how would you find your phone?"

"Dude, you're not as smart about hiding places as you think you are," Misha scoffs.

Tolya studies him with narrowed eyes, trying to figure out if he's bluffing or not.

"But also," Misha says, rushing ahead before Tolya can call him on it, "are we hosting a dinner party or something? It looks like you bought out the whole store."

"I just needed to get the stuff to make piroshki," Tolya says, turning back to start unloading the groceries. "And we were out of Gatorade, and rice—"

Misha makes some kind of noise that has Tolya's head snapping around, trying to find the source of the problem. "You're making piroshki? What's wrong?"

"Nothing's wrong," Tolya says, but his voice sounds weird and false even to his own ears. "I was just hungry and I haven't had piroshki in months, so I had my mom text me the recipe. You don't have to eat them if you don't want."

"Nope, nuh-uh," Misha says. "You told me, back when we first moved in together, you said your favorite food was your grandmother's piroshki, but that they were a lot of work, so you only make them when you feel upset or sad. So something made you upset or sad. What is it?"

Shit, Tolya thinks, shoving the last of the perishables into the fridge and closing the door, trying to buy himself time. But he knows Misha; he's like a dog with a bone. He's not going to let this go without a pretty significant distraction.

The sudden epiphany isn't accompanied by a beam of light or a choir of angels, but it might as well be. "Actually," he says, moving slowly across the kitchen until he has Misha backed up against the counter, barely a breath of space between their bodies. "I was thinking that maybe piroshki would be the perfect after-sex food."

Misha looks like he's about to protest, so Tolya pulls out the big guns. Sliding to his knees, he looks up at Misha from under his lashes, nudging the waist of his basketball shorts downward just a fraction.

"Your knee—" Misha begins, but the protest is half-hearted at best, especially given the way his cock is already taking an interest in the proceedings, clearly visible through the thin fabric of his shorts.

"Then we'll have to make this quick, won't we?" Tolya asks, pulling the shorts down further. "Unless—we don't have to if you don't want—"

Misha brushes back the bits of hair falling in his eyes, his left hand clumsy against Tolya's forehead. "I want, believe me. But you don't have to—"

"So neither of us have to, but both of us want to," Tolya interrupts, returning his attention to actually taking Misha's shorts off instead of just teasing him. Of course, that's when he discovers that Misha apparently decided to go without underwear today, his cock bobbing free as the shorts fall to the floor. "Fuck."

"I thought that was the idea," Misha teases, the shy note in his voice belying the boldness of his words.

Tolya doesn't waste any more time, partly because

Misha wasn't wrong about his knee. But mostly it's because he suddenly can't think of anything he wants more than to get his mouth on Misha, to take him apart and leave him shaken and sated, right here, right now.

"Oh, fuck," Misha groans. His free hand goes back to grip the edge of the counter, his thighs shaking under Tolya's hands. "God—fuck—Tolya, your mouth—"

Encouraged by the stream of disjointed curses and praise slipping from Misha's lips, Tolya devotes all of his attention to the task at hand, determined to get Misha off as quickly as possible. Thankfully Misha's cock isn't overly long, just enough to fill his mouth, but thick enough to stretch his lips satisfyingly.

Tolya bobs his head as quickly as he can, swirling his tongue around the shaft with every stroke. It doesn't take long before Misha starts moving, his hips thrusting just a little into Tolya's mouth, his voice getting more and more strained. "Tolya, fuck—I'm—I'm gonna—"

Gauging his moment, Tolya pulls off, stroking his hand over Misha's cock just as he starts to come. Last time he was too preoccupied with reaching his goal to really pay attention, but today, despite the slight warning twinge in his knee and the insistent throb of blood in his own cock, he's a little more clear-headed. He can notice the way Misha's teeth dig into his lower lip just before his mouth falls open, the way his whole body shakes with the force of his orgasm, the slick sheen of sweat covering his skin.

He doesn't stop stroking until his hand is slick and coated, until Misha is tugging ineffectively at him with his one good hand. "C'mere," he mutters, his words a little slurred and come-drunk. "I'ma get you."

"I have an idea," Tolya says hesitantly, but he lets himself be pulled to his feet, guides their lips together for a kiss when Misha leans in. "If you're cool with it."

"Honestly, right now I'm pretty much cool with anything," Misha says, smiling sweetly at him.

The sincerity of it hits Tolya like a punch to the gut, the trust that Misha is just handing him. "I—uh—would it be cool if I fuck your thighs?"

"Oh! Sure," Misha says, turning around and bracing his arms on the counter. "Like this?"

"Uh, yeah," Tolya says, pushing his sweats and underwear down with his clean hand. His cock bobs free eagerly, like it knows what's coming and is just waiting for him to get with the program.

He slicks himself up with his wet hand, shuddering a little at the sensation. When he looks up again, Misha is looking back over his shoulder, his legs spread just slightly.

It hits Tolya, then, the realization that he gets to do this. He gets to see Misha like this, soft and pliant in the aftermath of sex, gets to admire the muscled expanse of his back and the firm, round curve of his ass. It should feel strange, different. But it doesn't.

"What are you waiting for, an invitation?" Misha interrupts his reverie, smiling at him.

Unable to resist that smile, Tolya answers with actions rather than words, stepping closer and steadying himself with one hand on Misha's waist. Reaching between Misha's thighs, he slicks the skin as best he can before guiding his cock into the hot, tight space.

He's never really done this before, but it's so good he knows immediately that he's going to want to do it again. Everything is *hot slick tight* and when Misha flexes, squeezing his thighs together just a bit more, Tolya thinks he might die on the spot. And then he starts thrusting, just little movements at first, and it's somehow even better.

"Oh, God," he says, getting hold of Misha's waist with both hands for more leverage, only barely remembering to pull him back so he doesn't hit the counter with each thrust. "God, Misha—feels so good—I'm gonna."

"Yeah," Misha breathes, looking back over his shoulder. "C'mon, come all over me—"

Tolya maybe whites out a little when he comes. He's not sure, because he can't remember exactly. By the time his brain comes back online, he's slumped against Misha's back, pressing clumsy kisses to his shoulder and neck.

"Shit," he says, suddenly realizing that he's forcing Misha to hold up his weight. Straightening up so fast he swears he hears his back crack with the force of it, he urges Misha to turn around. "I'm sorry, are you okay? Did I—"

"I'm fine," Misha says, laughing. "But I want it on record that I'm not cleaning the jizz off the cabinets."

Tolya's face goes hot when he looks down to see, yeah, a stream of thick white fluid dripping down the front of the cabinet and puddling on the floor. "Yeah, I—I'll get that. You should go sit down, or lie down, probably—"

"I was thinking shower," Misha says, stretching slowly,

like a cat, his muscles rippling in a way that would have Tolya getting hard again if he hadn't literally just come. "But you should join me. For safety."

It takes some blinking, but eventually Tolya manages to get his brain back online. "Uh, yeah. Just give me a sec, I'll be right there."

"My hero," Mikey says, making a sad attempt to flutter his lashes.

Oh shit, Tolya realizes as he turns, blindly opening a cabinet that definitely doesn't contain cleaning supplies. *I'm in love with him.*

It takes him five cabinets before he remembers where they keep the bleach wipes.

Two weeks into the season

"Guess what?" Sunshine doesn't wait for an answer as he plops down next to them. "The internet thinks you two are dating."

"The internet has a brain now?" Tolya asks, cutting off another bite of his hotel omelet.

Sunshine rolls his eyes. "Don't play dumb with me. You may not be a college boy like me and Mikey, but I know you know what I'm talking about."

Mikey blinks at them, then down at the coffee cup in front of him, like figuring out how to get the cup to his mouth is too hard to figure out first thing in the morning. "Huh?"

"Here," Sunshine says, pulling his phone out of his pocket.

He unlocks it and sets it down in front of Tolya and Mikey. "Feel free to keep scrolling."

Tolya doesn't mean to read it. But his eyes move automatically over the lines of text, his brain comprehending without his permission. "Wha—is this a coffeeshop au?"

"Ha!" Sunshine says with his mouth full of disgusting, half-chewed oatmeal, pointing his spoon at Tolya. "I knew you knew about this nerd stuff."

"It's n—" Tolya cuts off the automatic defense. That's not the point. "Someone is writing fic about us?"

Thankfully Sunshine swallows before answering. "Not someone. Lots of someones. There are like thirty on this site."

"What's fic?" Mikey asks, because of course he picks now to join the conversation.

"Stories," Sunshine says gleefully. "About you two falling in loooooooveeeeee."

Mikey blinks at him, the gears starting to turn behind his eyes. "Me and Tolly? But we're not—"

"I know that," Sunshine says. "You know that. Tolly knows that. But the fans, they see what they want to see. And apparently what they see is sweet schoolboy romance. Or, you know, dirty locker room fucking. Take your pick."

"Sunshine!" Angel calls before they can get any deeper in this, thank fuck. "Get over here and quit traumatizing the rookies."

Grinning, Sunshine scoops up his phone, either not hearing or ignoring Tolya's stifled noise of protest. "Gotta go. You're welcome."

No matter the face he has to put on for the media sometimes, Mikey isn't stupid. Okay, yes, he got a little distracted by that blowjob, and the shower after, and then it was time for food. But, seriously, he defies anyone not to get distracted by Tolya's mouth. Or his hands. Or his cooking, for that matter—the piroshki really were the perfect after-sex food.

But then they move into the living room to digest, Tolya sprawling on the couch. And Mikey automatically moves to turn on the little clock radio he broke down and started listening to during the day, because seriously, the boredom struggle is super fucking real.

"—but if the Abs trade Michaelson—" is the first thing he hears. Because of course it is. And as if the gut-punch of the words isn't enough, he feels rather than sees

Tolya flinch out of the corner of his eye, surging to his feet and crossing the room to turn the radio off again.

"Something you want to tell me?" Mikey asks, unable to keep the bitterness out of his voice as he crosses to the couch. He feels like a teenager again, and not in a good way, unable to do anything but pout and whine about the unfairness of life, the universe and everything, while the adults only tell him what they want him to know.

Tolya shakes his head, sitting down more carefully than Mikey had. "It's just stupid rumors. Not even big ones. Just some bloggers."

"And local radio DJs," Mikey points out. "So clearly it's getting some traction."

"They're not gonna trade you," Tolya says fiercely. "We have plenty of cap space, the lines are solid, and you're the only guy on IR. We're actually doing really good on injuries for this time of the season."

Mikey wants to call Tolya on the thread of uncertainty in his voice, the way he won't quite meet his gaze. Any other time he would. But—

But he's injured, and he has no idea how long it'll be until he gets to play again, or even if he'll get to play again this season. But he knows the stubborn set of Tolya's jaw means that he's not prepared to give in, regardless of how correct the other party is. But he's tired, suddenly, bone-deep exhaustion that he hasn't felt in so long he can't remember.

"I think I'm gonna take a nap," he says, shoving himself up off the couch. He waits to hear Tolya say something, or come after him. Right now the only thing he wants more than his bed is for Tolya to wrap around him, to protect him from reality, just for a little while.

He's still waiting when the door of his bedroom closes behind him.

WHEN MIKEY WAKES up and wanders out into the living area, only to find it dark and deserted, he's disoriented for a minute, wondering if he forgot about a game. He reaches for his phone to check the schedule when reality sets in. He has no idea where Tolya hid his phone, or where Tolya is.

Moping his way into the kitchen for a drink, he finds a note stuck to the fridge with the Elsa magnet his sisters had bought him as a housewarming present. *Children's hospital visits*, it says. *Back by 5 probably.*

He stands there for probably a ridiculous amount of time staring at Tolya's scribbled signature—why did this dork think he had to sign a note when they're literally the only two people in this apartment? Finally he remembers why he came in the kitchen in the first place, grabbing a cup out of the dishwasher and filling it from the dispenser in the fridge door.

It's a bad idea. He knows this, but he finds himself drawn to the radio with an almost magnetic pull. The combined rush of relief and disappointment when he turns it on to the latest Ariana Grande song is so strong it's almost sickening.

Then, because he can't leave well enough alone, he hits the tuner button, moving through the frequencies until he hits the sports talk station. They're on commercial break, of course, but he leaves it there, slouching down on the couch with his water bottle, and waits.

Because this is Edmonton, once the DJs come back on, he doesn't have to wait long before the conversation turns to hockey. The Abs have been frustratingly mediocre this season, and of course everyone has an opinion on this. He gets so caught up in arguing with people who can't hear him that he almost forgets what he was expecting.

Of course, that's when it hits him. "And with Michaelson still on IR, we aren't the only people wondering if the Abs will trade him before the deadline. So far the speculation is limited to a few individual blogs, but as the deadline approaches, it will probably heat up. Let's take some calls. Sandra from Leduc, what do you think?"

"I don't think they should trade him," the tinny voice says.

"I love you, Sandra," Mikey crows, pumping his left arm.

Meanwhile the host says, "Oh, really?"

"Michaelson has been really strong this season, and he and Petrov play better together than apart. But I think they might end up sending him down for the rest of the season and keeping Carson."

Mikey groans. "Boo, Sandra."

"Thanks for calling," the host says. "Let's take another caller. Walter from Lodgepole, should the Abs trade Michaelson?"

"AB-solutely," the man says, leaning on the first syllable, his tone making it clear he's waiting for the DJ to chuckle. "It's his rookie year, fourth-line d-men are a dime a dozen. We'd probably have to trade someone else or a good draft pick along with him to get someone worthwhile, but he's not doing us any good sitting on his ass in IR."

Mikey rolls his eyes. "Fuck you, Walter."

He really, literally is sitting on his ass at this moment, and suddenly he can't stand it any longer. It's probably too soon, but the neurologist had just said he had to wait another week for formal physiotherapy, not simple exercise.

It feels good to stand up, change the station to something with loud, driving music, and drop into a squat. His muscles feel almost relieved when he repeats the motion, like all the energy he hasn't been using was stored just for this moment. When he starts to feel the burn in his quads, he stretches out on the floor, tucking his feet under the edge of the couch, and rips out a set of sit-ups instead.

He moves through as many exercises as he can think of that don't require two hands: lunges, clumsy jumping jacks, one-handed push-ups and planks, then starts over again. Every time he starts to think about getting traded, or sent down, he moves faster, pushes harder.

Within an embarrassingly short period of time, he's gasping for breath and covered in sweat, lying flat on the floor and staring at the ceiling.

Naturally, this is when Tolya comes through the door.

"Misha? What happened? Do we need to call—"

"I'm fine," Mikey says, lifting a hand to cut him off and doing his best to ignore the warm feeling in his chest when Tolya calls him "Misha." "Just did a little exercise, see where I'm at before I start physio next week."

Tolya doesn't seem entirely convinced, but when Mikey sits up and then stands unassisted, he looks a little less crazy around the eyes. "And you're okay?"

Mikey barely suppresses the urge to roll his eyes. "I'm fine, see?"

He wasn't expecting the way Tolya's eyes darken as they follow his gesturing hand down the line of his body. Somehow, the idea that Tolya might actually want him, that he's doing this thing they're doing because he wants to, hasn't really occurred to Mikey before. But there's no mistaking the look on his face.

"I can see that," Tolya says, his voice a little rough.

"But I'm all sweaty," Mikey says—yeah, it's cheesy to lift up his t-shirt and wipe his forehead, but sue him. Not much else has made him feel good lately. "I need a shower. Someone should come with me to make sure I don't fall and hurt myself."

Tolya grins wryly. "Someone, huh? Out of all the people here?"

"I mean, if you don't wanna—"

"I didn't say that," Tolya says hastily, crossing the room and nudging Mikey toward the hallway. "Let's go get you cleaned up."

Mikey still has no idea what this thing that they're doing is, but he's not going to question it right now.

"MIKEY!" Guns booms as soon as Tolya opens the apartment door, pushing his way inside. "Good to fucking see you, dude!"

"You too," Mikey says, surprised by how much he means it. He hadn't realized until now just how fucking weird it was, going weeks without seeing or talking to anybody on the team but Tolya. And this isn't the whole team, of course. But with Orange, Sunshine, and Angel following Guns into the apartment, he feels something inside him relaxing.

By the time Nova, Pigeon, Gonzo, and Rover have piled in, showing up with various beverages alcoholic and non, he's actually feeling the best he has since his injury. The living area is full of chatter, conversations happening in English, Spanish, and Russian all at once, and the pizzas Tolya ordered show up just in time. It feels good. It feels like home.

"Seriously, mijo, how are you doing?" Sunshine asks, cornering him in the kitchen when he goes to grab a soda, doing his best not to eye the beers longingly.

"You're like, three years older than me," Mikey

complains, cracking open the can. "You're not my real dad."

Sunshine rolls his eyes. "Fine, 'nito. Humor an old man."

"I'm good," Mikey says. In this moment, it's true. Sunshine, on the other hand, looks a little off, the corners of his mouth tight, his smile a little too wide "Are you okay?"

"Why wouldn't I be?" Sunshine asks, like that's a real answer.

Before Mikey can dig any deeper, Tolya comes around the end of the counter, digging in the fridge for a beer. "You doing okay, Misha?"

Nova raises his eyebrows obnoxiously at them from the barstool where he's perched.

Mikey's face heats. "I'm fine," he answers, doing his best not to snap.

"Do you think we should order more pizza?" Tolya asks, poking through the empty boxes spread across the counter.

The good news is that the resulting debate completely distracts anyone who might have wanted to dig into Tolya's new nickname for him. Mikey's not stupid, he knows his mom bribed Pigeon, Gonzo, and Sunshine to keep tabs on him with the promise of homemade tamales, and Nova and Rover are almost certainly doing the same for Tolya's dad. They got off light, really. The bad news is that nobody gives into his request to order just one more supreme.

It's not that he wants to keep this whatever-it-is between him and Tolya secret, Mikey rationalizes as he gets roped into a game of Cards Against Humanity with Rover's gross custom deck. It's just—it feels delicate. Private. And that's nice.

This whole evening is nice, actually. Mikey feels just a little high on how much fun he's having, even though he isn't allowed to drink right now. He's surrounded by his team, his head doesn't hurt, but his stomach does a little, from laughing at the dirty jokes generated by the game. And every now and then he catches Tolya's eye and sees a look that makes him think maybe, once everyone's gone, he won't be sleeping alone.

Of course, that's when everything goes to shit.

Guns draws a new white card and does a weird, full-body flinch. "I need a different card," he says quietly, or as quietly as he's capable of talking. Which of course, draws more attention.

"No way," Orange complains. "You don't get to just switch out cards because you don't like 'em. Even if Rover is a disgusting motherfucker."

"Fine," Guns says reluctantly. "Let's play."

Pigeon leans over and grabs the card before Guns can react. "Let's see what's so bad," he crows, throwing it down in the middle of the table as Guns lunges ineffectually after him.

Mikey thinks absently that he's never heard this group of guys so quiet before, or seen everyone freeze like they do in the movies. But most of his attention is caught by the card lying there. Four words, in stark black on the white background.

The CHL Trade Deadline.

Everything starts back up again suddenly, Rover scooping the card up and shoving it back in the box, Angel tossing out a new black card for everyone to match. Everyone else is talking, a little too loudly, a little too cheerfully, ignoring the elephant in the room.

It's suddenly all too much, and Mikey pushes back from the table, setting his cards down. "Bathroom," he says, probably not convincing anyone, but they'll all pretend. It's what they do. "Play this round without me."

Just like every game, he thinks bitterly as he escapes.

No one comes after him. Just like he wants it.

Three days after moving in

"Yeah, Mom," Mikey says. He has to suppress a groan when he accidentally pushes too hard with the lacrosse ball he's using to massage his quads. "I think you'll like the apartment. It's really nice, and close to the arena, so we won't have far to drive."

"That sounds good, mijo," she says, keyboard clicking away on the other end of the call. "And it's not too expensive? You think you and Tolly will do okay as roommates?"

Mikey forces himself not to cross his fingers. It's not a lie. The apartment isn't too expensive. For him. Even a rookie

CHL salary is more money than his parents make in five years. He's trying not to think about it. "No, it's right in the middle of our price range. And yeah, I think Tolly's gonna be a great roommate."

"He can't be worse than that boy your freshman year, I guess," his mom says."

Shuddering at the memory of his freshman year roommate and the biohazard that was their room, Mikey switches to his other thigh. "Exactly. Tolly's a nice guy. You'll like him. I think we're actually gonna be friends."

The typing pauses for a second before resuming. "That's great, Kevin. Just remember, you have to communicate."

"We're moving in together, not dating."

"Sometimes that's harder," *she says, her voice serious.* "Without sex as a distraction—"

"Mom!" *His face goes hot. He's so grateful Tolly isn't around to hear even his side of the conversation.*

She sighs. "I'm just saying, mijo, it sounds like you two work well together on the ice. But you can't expect him to read your mind. Don't do the thing where you assume someone knows what you want and then pout because you didn't get it."

"I don't pout," *he mutters.*

"Oh, you absolutely do," *she says cheerfully.* "Remember. Honest communication. Tell him what you want him to do. You might be surprised how often you get it."

He rolls his eyes, then winces like she can see it through the phone somehow. "I'm hanging up now."

"Bien. Te amo, mijito."

"Tu también, mamá."

After the call ends, he thinks for a moment, then texts Andrea, Do I pout?

Does a bear shit in the woods? *Her reply is almost instantaneous.* ur pout would make drag queens jealous

"What's up?" Tolly asks, coming in the door of their hotel room and getting a look at him.

Mikey shakes his head, setting his phone aside. "My family is the worst."

"But you love them," Tolya says after studying his face for a minute.

"Yeah," he says, his mouth curling up in a smile despite himself. "Yeah, I do."

11

Tolya knows Misha isn't really going to the bathroom; everyone knows that, but they're all pretending to buy the excuse. Right now he can't think of anything he wants more than to chase after Misha, to distract him or cheer him up or, fuck, just be with him. Because he's hurting, and not being there to help is one of the hardest things Tolya's ever done.

God, he's in so fucking deep.

But they have an apartment full of hockey players, so now isn't the time for introspection, or for following Misha around like a lovesick puppy. Nova's raised eyebrows over his "Misha" earlier is going to be the least of the chirps if the team figures out that they're—that they're fucking. Not that Tolya's embarrassed by it, by Misha. But if Rover or Nova or, God help him, Trout, figure out that he's gone and fallen in love with his d-partner—

Tolya shudders. The only thing that spreads through the CHL faster than rumors is actual, juicy gossip. He'd have maybe 5 hours at most before his dad cals Misha to give him a shovel talk and the whole thing blows up.

It's not like he's embarrassed or ashamed. He just wants a little more time, a little longer where it's just them.

So he doesn't go after him. When Misha's been gone half an hour, though, he starts herding everyone out of the apartment. To their credit, they go without much protest, although Angel does steal the last of the pizza, because he's a dick like that.

"Just leave already," Tolya says, shoving him toward the door.

"Fine, I'm going, I'm going," Angel says, hugging the pizza box protectively to his chest.

The rest of the guys follow him out, with Rover bringing up the rear. He pauses next to Tolya, waving Nova ahead of him. "I'm not going to ask," he says in Russian, lowering his voice. "You two just take care of each other, okay?"

Tolya blinks at him, startled. "I—"

"Not asking," Rover repeats, clapping him on the shoulder. "See you at practice."

Closing the door behind them, Tolya does his best to shake off the surprise. Whatever Rover knows, or thinks he knows, isn't important right now. What's important is Misha.

He locks the front door and heads for Misha's room, hesitating just outside. In the face of the closed bedroom door, all his self-doubts rise up to choke him. Maybe Misha doesn't want him there. Maybe Misha really does want to be alone. Maybe, probably, what they're doing is just sex, and probably Tolya's an idiot who went and caught feelings.

Just as he's about to turn around, the door opens. "Hey—" he starts, only to cut off when he sees the pinched look on Misha's face. "Headache?"

"Yeah," Misha whispers.

"Go lay down again, I'll get your meds," Tolya orders. "Or do you want to be on the couch?"

Misha hesitates for a moment. "The guys?"

"They're gone," Tolya says, steadying Misha with a hand on his elbow. "Couch or bed?"

"Couch," Misha says, walking toward the living area with exaggerated care.

It seems to take forever to retrieve the Tylenol, to bring it and a glass of water to the couch while trying to avoid unnecessary noise. Misha takes it gratefully when he gets there, though, swallowing gingerly and curling up in the corner of the couch while Tolya sets the water within easy reach.

"Do you want to be by yourself?" Tolya asks as quietly as he can. "Or—"

"Or," Misha interrupts. "By myself sucks."

Tolya does his best to remind himself that it doesn't necessarily mean anything; just because Misha doesn't want to be alone doesn't mean he wants Tolya's company specifically. But that doesn't erase the warm glow in his chest at the words, or when Misha barely waits until he's sat down before leaning over and curling into his body.

He has no idea how long they sit like that. It's oddly soothing, no TV, no phone, just the sound of their breathing slowly syncing up, the low hum of traffic from outside the apartment, the refrigerator motor running in the kitchen.

Finally, though Misha sits up straight with a sigh.

"Better?" Tolya asks, fighting the urge to pull him back in.

"Yeah," Misha says slowly, rolling his head from side to side. "But now my neck and shoulders are super tight. Maybe I'll come to practice with you in the morning, see if I can beg Sara for some massage and hot tub time."

Tolya nods. "Sounds good. But I could try to help you with that, if you want?"

Misha blinks at him. "You don't have to. I can make it to tomorrow, no problem—"

"If you don't want me to, that's cool—" Tolya mumbles, his face heating. Of course Misha would rather wait for a professional.

"No, no," Misha interrupts, taking his hand. "I just— you're already doing so fucking much, Tolya, and I—I'm just laying around being useless. I don't want you to feel like you have to take care of me."

Tolya shakes his head, doing his best not to read too much into the fact that Misha is calling him "Tolya" instead of "Tolly." "I like taking care of you," he says quietly, squeezing Misha's hand gently. "Back in Juniors, they called me 'Mom' half the time."

"And here I thought I was special," Misha says, but his teasing tone falls a little flat, and he starts to withdraw his hand.

"You are," Tolya blurts out, tightening his grip and trying not to panic over the words that escaped, rushing ahead before Misha can comment. "Come on, let me try. If it doesn't help, I'll stop."

Misha eyes him closely. "Yeah, okay. If you're sure."

"I'll be right back," Tolya says. "Don't move, okay? Well, actually, we should probably do this on a bed so I can really get to your shoulders."

"Make up your mind," Misha replies, laughing a little. "Am I staying here, or going to a bed?"

Tolya reaches down and pulls him to his feet. "My bed," he says. "Come on."

Misha grins at him. "I see how it is."

"I mean, if you don't want a massage," Tolya says, pretending to let go of his hand.

"No, no, I want it," Misha says, holding on tightly. "Take me to bed and rub your hands all over me."

Tolya rolls his eyes. "I hate you."

"No you don't," Misha says, following him into his room.

"No, I don't," Tolya agrees. "Take your shirt off, I'll be right back."

He doesn't wait for a response, heading into his bathroom to dig through the drawers and cabinets until —"Aha!" he says, grabbing the bottle of massage oil. "I knew I had this somewhere. Why are you still wearing a shirt?"

"Broken arm?" Misha says, gesturing demonstratively with his cast. "The important question is, why do you have massage oil? Did you date someone who was into that? Why didn't I know about this?"

"Sara gave it to me so I could work on my knee myself," Tolya says, trying to convince himself there wasn't a jealous note in Misha's voice at the mention of him dating someone. Tossing the bottle and the towels he'd taken from the bathroom onto the bed, he reaches for the hem of Misha's t-shirt.

It's ridiculous to be so distracted by Misha's eyes, he tells himself firmly. They're brown eyes. Very nice brown eyes, but he's not the kind of guy to get poetic over someone's eyes, for fuck's sake. Thankfully, working Misha's shirtsleeve down over the cast to finish taking his shirt off gives him a reason to look away before he embarrasses himself.

"Okay," he says, glancing back up. "Let me spread out the towels so we—"

Misha's hand on the back of his neck is clumsy, but Tolya goes willingly into the kiss. Unlike the other times they've kissed, it's not hot and frantic, not a stop on the rush toward orgasm. They're both turned on; he can feel Misha half-hard against him, the answering throb of blood in his cock when Misha nips lightly at his lower lip.

Despite all that, the kiss is slow and lazy, almost soft. Tolya doesn't want to stop, wants to keep kissing and kissing for as long as they can. But then Misha goes to tilt his head and flinches back from the kiss, making a quiet, pained noise against Tolya's lips.

"Come on, let me try to help," Tolya says, forcing himself to let go and turn toward the bed. Pulling the comforter and top sheet down and spreading out the towels only takes a few minutes, and then he's ready.

When he turns back, Misha is completely naked, kicking his feet free of his boxers. "How are we doing this?" he asks.

Tolya does his best to swallow his already-instinctive reaction to being faced with a naked Misha, especially when he doesn't even need to be completely naked for a neck and shoulder rub. But hell, it's not like they don't both know where this is going. "Sit down first," he says, picking up the bottle of massage oil and climbing onto the mattress. "Let me work on your neck without your head being turned. Then you can lie down while I get your shoulders."

"Yes, sir," Misha says, sticking out his tongue as he sits down with his back toward Tolya.

"Hey, I'm trying to do you a favor here," Tolya says, but there's no heat in it. They both know he's not going to stop. Even if they weren't whatever they are, he wouldn't leave Misha in this kind of pain if he could help it.

Everything else aside, it's kind of magic, watching Misha slowly go soft and pliant under his hands. Tolya takes his time, watching closely to see when he's doing more harm than good, when he presses too hard and Misha tenses up under it, ruining the effect of the massage.

It takes a few minutes of focused attention, but eventually the muscles in Misha's neck are loose and warm. When Tolya prompts him, he can turn his head from side to side without wincing.

"Magic hands," Misha says, stretching his arms above his head. "Want me to lay down now?"

"Yeah, go ahead and get comfortable," Tolya says.

Misha snorts out a laugh. His cock bobs in midair as he crawls onto the bed, fully hard and gorgeous. "Not sure how well that's going to work."

"We can take a break if you want," Tolya offers half-heartedly.

"Are you kidding?" Mikey stretches out, adjusting himself and settling onto the towels with a sigh. "I'm not turning down a free massage."

It only takes a couple of minutes before Tolya decides that trying to work the knots out of Misha's shoulder while sitting next to him is for the birds. "Brace yourself," he warns, stripping out of his jeans before climbing up to straddle Misha's waist.

"You're heavy," Misha says, in a voice that doesn't sound like a complaint.

"Free massage," Tolya reminds him, pouring out more oil into his palms, indulging himself by running his hands slowly up Misha's back before returning to his shoulders.

It's nice, getting to just touch him like this. It's hot, for sure, the little noises Misha makes, the way he all but melts into the mattress, the way his muscles flex and relax under Tolya's hands. But it's also just intimate, in a non-sexual way. The basic contact of skin on skin, getting to let his hands roam wherever he wants, is a simple pleasure he didn't know he wanted until he had it.

Eventually, though, just as Tolya's erection is getting more insistent, Misha turns his head and says "You can fuck me. I mean, if you want."

Tolya swears his brain crashes like a computer for a few seconds. "I—you—really?"

Misha shrugs a shoulder, the muscles of his back rippling under Tolya's hands where they stopped. "We don't have to if you don't want. I'm cool with whatever."

"I—fuck, I want that. What do you want?" Tolya counters. "This isn't just your weird thing about orgasm equality, is it?"

"First of all, it's not weird," Misha says. "I'm not going to be the kind of dick who goes around talking about how he gets head but doesn't give it back. That's bullshit. And secondly—no. I—I've been thinking about it."

Tolya has to reach down then, has press a hand against where his cock strains against the fabric of his boxers, just to relieve the pressure. "Yeah?"

"Yeah," Misha breathes, his hips moving a little. Like he's grinding into the mattress, like imagining it, talking about it is turning him on just as much as it is Tolya. "I try not to think about it too much, since I can't jerk off. But I—I want to."

"Tell me," Tolya coaxes. He gets his hands moving again, but this time there's no pretense of massaging. This time he's just touching to touch, to feel. "What do you think about? Like this, with me behind you?"

Misha sucks in a deep, shuddering breath. "Sometimes," he says, his voice quiet. "Sometimes with you behind me, but we're up on our knees. Or sometimes I'm on top, or you are, but with me on my back. And—"

Tolya waits, but there doesn't seem to be any more forthcoming. "And?" he prompts.

"And sometimes I'm fucking you," Misha says, all in a rush. Like he's not sure what Tolya will think, will say.

"We are definitely doing that," Tolya says fervently, sliding off and to the side. He takes advantage of his new access to Misha's ass, stroking his hand over the muscular curve while digging through his bedside table drawer for lube and praying he still has condoms.

Misha watches him, eyes bright, lower lip caught between his teeth. "Yeah? You'd be—you'd want that?"

I can't imagine not wanting you, Tolya thinks, holds the too-honest words between his teeth as he finds a condom packet. "That sounds fucking hot," he says instead. "Did you want to tonight?" He has practice in the morning, but he's not about to point that out. Not when this moment feels fragile, almost, like the wrong word or movement could shatter it.

"Nah," Misha says, his face almost shy. "Not tonight."

"Okay," Tolya says, not wanting to push. Picking up the lube and condom, he shifts back to sit on the bed, nudging Misha's legs apart to make room. "It's, uh, been awhile since I've done this."

Misha shrugs, one hand picking at a frayed corner of the towel underneath him. "Well, it's been never since I've done this, so you're ahead of me."

Tolya just barely manages not to drop the lube in his surprise. "I thought—didn't you say you'd had a boyfriend in college?"

"Yeah, but Sam didn't like, uh—"

"Penetration?" Tolya supplies.

Misha nods. "So yeah, all new to me."

Tolya opens the lube, drizzling it over his fingers. "Okay, just tell me if something hurts. We can take our time."

"Speak for yourself," Misha mutters. But he pulls his knees up under him when Tolya suggests it, shivers at the first brush of Tolya's fingers over his hole.

"Did you ever do this to yourself?" Tolya asks, making teasing circles over the tight furl. "Before your arm?"

Misha shrugs, his eyelashes fluttering against his cheekbones. "Tried a couple of times. I don't think I was doing it right, though. It just felt weird."

"It takes some practice," Tolya agrees, rubbing his free hand up and down over Misha's ass cheek, spreading him open wider. "Or toys. I recommend toys."

"Never got the hang of it, even with toys. Maybe—"

Misha's breath catches, his hips rocking back into Tolya's touch. "Maybe you could show me, sometime."

Tolya swallows hard, his imagination all too ready to take the current situation and paint a vivid mental picture. Misha writhing and gorgeous as Tolya works a plug into his ass, as Tolya fucks him with a dildo, coming untouched. "Yeah, we could try that if you want. Now?"

Misha shakes his head, his eyes flying open. "No, not —not this time."

"You want my cock first?" Tolya asks, using the distraction to press his fingertip just inside. It's hard to concentrate, but he forces himself to go slow. Misha needs him to do this right.

"Yeah," Misha says on a shaky sigh. "I think so."

Tolya bites his lip, the sharp sting helping him focus on something besides his erection, than imagining what it would be like to push inside Misha with more than just one finger. It's been a long time since he's felt this strung out, this turned on.

"This okay?" he asks once his finger is sliding in as far as it will go, moving in and out without significant resistance, Misha squirming a little under his touch.

"I—yeah," Misha says. "It doesn't hurt."

Despite everything, Tolya can't help but smile. He turns his hand, crooks his fingers, searching. "Still just weird?"

Misha's tone is very unconvincing when he says. "It's fine, it's good. You can—fuck!"

Tolya grins wider, dragging his fingertip over the same spot again. "You were saying?"

"Holy fuck," Misha pants, fucking himself back on Tolya's finger, trying to get more stimulus on his prostate.

Either the second and third fingers go faster or Tolya slips into kind of a zen state, balanced forever on the edge of arousal. It seems like only a few minutes before he's thrusting three fingers in and out, watching the way Misha's whole body reacts.

"If you don't get in me soon I'm gonna come," Misha pants, his forehead pressed to the mattress.

"Don't you want to come?" Tolya asks.

Misha literally fucking growls, like maybe he's wound as tightly as Tolya. "I. Want. You. To. Fuck. Me," he says, each word spaced out.

"Whatever you want," Tolya promises.

He's too far gone to worry about how sincere it sounds, how much he means it. Right now all he can focus on is getting the condom packet open, rolling it over his hard, leaking cock. Doing it one-handed is tricky, but he manages.

Misha makes a small, protesting noise when Tolya pulls his fingers free. Even through the latex of the condom, spreading more lube over his cock feels unbelievably good. He shudders, his eyes sliding closed for a second.

"C'mon," Misha says, looking back over his shoulder. "Tolya—"

"I've got you," Tolya promises, lining himself up and pushing inside.

Even with what felt like a subjective eternity of prep, Misha's body is hot and tight around him. He has to force himself to take it slow, fighting the instinct to just push in past the resistance.

"You good?" he asks hoarsely when he's as deep as he can go, his hipbones pressed to the curve of Misha's ass, his fingers flexing on Misha's waist.

"Gimme a minute," Misha replies, his voice similarly thready.

Tolya frees a hand, strokes it down his spine, as much because he can as to soothe. "Okay. Take as much time as you need."

Slowly, the tense line of Misha's back relaxes under his touch, his body curving back into the mattress. "Okay," Misha says, a long exhale. "I think—you can move now."

Despite the reassurance, despite the pounding of his pulse in his ears, in his chest, in his cock, Tolya starts slow —a tiny withdrawal, an equally tiny thrust in, watching all the while. But Misha doesn't tense again, just pushes back, silently asking for more.

"I'm not gonna last long," Tolya warns, deepening his next thrust.

"Me either," Misha says, his voice shaky. "Tolya, please—"

It takes him a few tries to find the right angle, but when he finally hits Misha's prostate he can see the shock of it roll through his body.

"Fuck," Misha moans, shaking under Tolya's hands. "Fuck, shit, fuckkk—"

Tolya holds onto control with his fingernails, every ounce of willpower focused on making sure Misha comes before he does. He's not at all sure he'll be able to manage it—every thrust feels better than the last, the tight, slick warmth of Misha's body around him so good, so right, he never wants it to end.

Just when he's sure that he can't hold out any longer, that he's going to come, Misha's whole body goes taut under him. With the tight grip of Misha's ass on his cock, Tolya is helpless to do anything but follow, his hands tight around Misha's waist as he thrusts deep one last time.

He has no idea how long they stay like that, with him slumped bonelessly over Misha's back. Long enough that Misha finally mumbles something about him being heavy, recalling Tolya to the fact that he is, in fact, currently lying on top of his injured—best friend? Teammate? D-partner?

Setting aside for the moment the question of what, exactly, they are to each other, he forces himself up, disposing of the condom and getting a washcloth from the bathroom. When he returns to the bedroom, he's amused to find that the only movement Misha has made is to stretch his legs out behind him, leaving him completely flat on his stomach.

"Come on," he says, coaxing Misha off of the oil- and semen-stained towel and onto his back. "We need to clean this up before it gets stuck to you."

"Can't move,"Misha mumbles, throwing his good arm across his eyes.

Tolya shakes his head, wiping Misha down as best he can. "You'll feel better once you've showered."

"No shower. Sleep," Misha says, snuggling deeper into the mattress.

"Fine."

Tolya gathers up the towel and washcloth, taking them directly to the washing machine. There are some things he doesn't want to think about the housekeeping service finding. And it's not like he doesn't know how to do laundry.

When he returns to his room, he finds Misha sound asleep, soft snores coming from under the arm still covering his face. Tolya turns off the light and closes the door behind him, crossing the room in the dark and sliding into the bed.

He has to nudge Misha over a little to make room before he pulls the covers up from the foot of the bed and over them, half-expecting Misha to wake up and stumble off to his own bed. But all he does is snuggle close as soon as Tolya is settled in, wrapping around him like Tolya is the world's best stuffed animal.

For all the things they've done together so far, this is the first time they've literally slept together, Tolya realizes. He'd like to consider that more, to think about what it means, but the physical and emotional exhaustion of the day has him slipping into sleep himself.

When he wakes up in the morning, light glowing around the edge of the curtains, Misha still clinging like an octopus, Tolya realizes that he'd forgotten entirely about the trade rumors.

Second roadie of the season

"So yeah, Sam was great, but he didn't want to be a hockey boyfriend," Mikey says, a tinge of wistfulness coloring his otherwise matter-of-fact tone. Or maybe Tolya's imagining things; the hotel room is dark, and it's not like he can see Mikey's face well enough to tell. "What about you?"

Tolya shrugs, realizing at the last moment that Mikey can't see it, but the rustling of the sheets probably conveys the movement. "Nobody serious. I fooled around some in Juniors, you know, and there was a girl I hooked up with some last season, but—it's hard. When you don't know how long you're gonna be there. I kept kind of holding myself at arm's length. But she didn't want anything serious either; I don't think she really did relationships."

"It's hard," Mikey says. "With hockey."

"Yeah."

Silence hangs there between them for a moment, soft and sleepy. "Do you want that?" Mikey asks finally. "Like some-day? Husband or wife, kids, the whole shebang?"

"Yeah," Tolya admits. "I always wanted like, brothers or sisters, but my mom had such a hard time with me—I totally get why they didn't. But I want like, a lot of kids. At least three."

"If you think three is a lot, you'll have to meet my cousins someday," Mikey says with a soft laugh. "But yeah, me too. Someday. Probably after retirement, at this rate."

Tolya smiles into the darkness. "Listen to you. Just your rookie season and you're already giving up on relationships. One foot in the grave already."

Mikey snorts. "Yeah, yeah, whatever. But I get it, you know, why a lot of these guys marry their high school sweethearts. It's hard."

"Yeah," Tolya agrees again. It's still as true as the last time Mikey said it. "But you'll find somebody. When it's right."

"You, too," Mikey says, his voice cracking on a yawn in the middle of the last word.

It's the last thing Tolya hears before sliding down into sleep.

12

MIKEY

"Everything looks good," Dr. Chakravarthy the neurologist says, looking up at them with a smile from the computer where she's been reviewing the latest battery of tests. "You can start slowly adding screen time. No more than 30 minutes today, and you can add half an hour every day. But if it starts triggering headaches, call me and back it down, understand?"

Mikey nods enthusiastically. At this point, he's pretty sure he'd agree to stand on one foot, naked, in the waiting room if it got him his phone back. Well, maybe not naked.

Probably not naked.

"The orthopedist has cleared you for physiotherapy?" she asks, glancing back at her screen.

"Yeah, starting tomorrow," Mikey says, trying not to

bounce out of his chair at the prospect. Physio is gonna suck, he knows this. But he's starting to feel like all of the energy he would've used on hockey and workouts is just sitting in his muscles, buzzing like a swarm of bees, demanding to be used. Honestly, Tolya's hand on his knee is probably the only thing keeping him in his chair right now.

The doctor smiles like she can tell what he's thinking. Hell, maybe she can. "Good for you. Be careful not to overdo it; straining your body can also cause a recurrence of concussion symptoms. If that happens, tell your physio, but also call so we can check you out and make sure it's nothing serious."

"We will," Tolya promises, squeezing Mikey's knee. "Is there anything else we should look out for?"

Mikey maybe doesn't catch all of Dr. Chakravarthy's answer. But in his defense, the combination of Tolya's hand on his knee and Tolya's serious voice saying "we" like it means something—like they're together for real, not just teammates and d-partners and best buddies who fuck—

It's distracting, okay?

"—and you can always call if you have any questions," she's saying when Mikey finally tunes back in. "If I'm not available, the nurses can answer most things, and they can always find me or the neurologist on call in an emergency."

"Thank you," Tolya says, getting to his feet and holding out his hand to shake.

The doctor shakes it, then Mikey's hand when he

offers it. "You're very welcome. I'm glad to see you having such a quick recovery, Kevin. You're very lucky to have such a supportive partner to help you with it."

Out of the corner of his eye, he can see Tolya's face going pink. Not the red of total embarrassment, just a soft pink that makes Mikey think of cuddling, of waking up together, of Tolya's voice when he says "Misha."

"I really am," he agrees, smiling at Dr. Chakravarthy. The warmth in his chest just grows when Tolya doesn't correct her assumption, when Tolya's hand lands on the small of his back as they leave the office.

As soon as they're in the car, he turns to Tolya. "Okay! Phone time!"

"What makes you think I have your phone?" Tolya counters, fastening his seatbelt. "Plus you only get thirty minutes today. Do you really want to spend it on your phone?"

"Fuck yes I do," Mikey retorts, wiggling the fingers of his outstretched hand. "C'mon, Tolya, please?"

Tolya sighs, digging in his pocket and pulling out his phone. No, wait. Not his phone. That's Mikey's case, with the Abs Pride night sticker he'd put on there after he came out to his parents junior year.

"I knew it!" Mikey takes the phone, almost dropping it in his eagerness. Unlocking it is almost instant, pure muscle memory, and he doesn't realize until he's staring at the screen with all its colorful icons that he's braced, waiting for the stabbing pain inside his skull.

It doesn't come, though. Not the first second, or the

handful of heartbeats after it. Mikey lets out a breath he didn't realize he was holding, tapping on the Instagram icon and wincing a little at the number of notifications.

"Good?" Tolya asks.

Mikey looks up from the screen, melting a little at the familiar look of concern on Tolya's face. "Yeah, all good. No ice picks stabbing my skull, no brain explosions."

Tolya smiles back, putting the car in gear. "Good."

After a few seconds of checking his notifications, Mikey just gives up. There's too much, and he doesn't want to waste any of his limited minutes. Hitting the selfie camera, he tilts it so both he and Tolya are in the frame, captions it "back, baby!" and posts quickly.

The rest of the drive is more of the same, marking the untold notifications as read. It's only been a few weeks since his injury, but it's a little startling how many posts, how many things ranging from inane to life-changing he's missed. Like, he knows social media isn't life, obviously. But it's still weird.

Checking Deadspin is a dumbass idea, but somehow he finds himself there. And of course he's rewarded for his stupidity with a post about the likelihood of him getting traded. He taps on the headline like someone hypnotized, like he can't help himself, and starts reading, only to nearly jump out of his skin when Tolya yanks the phone from his hand.

"Don't," Tolya says quietly, closing the article and handing the phone back to him just as the light turns green.

"I want to know," Mikey answers, his voice just as quiet.

Tolya sighs. "There's knowing and then there's speculation on the internet. They're two different things. Don't do this to yourself, Misha. It's not going to get you back on the ice faster, or do anything besides make you worry."

"I'm already worried," Mikey says.

"I know."

They drive the rest of the way home in silence. Mikey starts to say something a few times, but always ends up closing his mouth before any words come out.

What would he say?

I'm scared that they'll trade me.

What if I never play again?

Are we dating?

As soon as they make it inside their apartment, he shoves Tolya back against the closed door, sliding to his knees in the same movement.

"Misha?" Tolya asks, reaching down to cover Mikey's good hand with his own where it's working on the button of his jeans. "You don't have to—"

"I want—" Mikey cuts off, all the things he wants rising up in his throat so fast he feels like they'll choke him. He can't have his arm healed, or ice time, or the certainty of not getting traded right now. But he can have this. "I want to. I want—"

"Okay, okay." Tolya lets go, his fingers running through Mikey's hair instead, his voice low and soothing. "Whatever you want, Misha."

I want to forget, Mikey thinks, pulling the zipper down, then dragging the waistband of Tolya's boxer briefs to let his cock spring free. Wrapping his hand around the base, he swallows as much of it as he can in one go, narrowing his focus until the only thing that matters is right now.

All there is is this moment. The slow pulse against his tongue as Tolya hardens in his mouth. The slide of skin under his lips as he moves. The little noises and bitten-off curses above him, the tremor in Tolya's thighs, the flex of his fingers against Mikey's skull.

"Fuck," Tolya gasps, low and urgent, thrusting just a little into Mikey's mouth. "Fuck, Misha—I—"

Mikey slides down as far as he can, until he feels the head of Tolya's cock bumping against his throat, his lips stretched wide around the base. The first swallow is involuntary, but when Tolya groans, he does it again on purpose, moving as fast as he can. He needs Tolya to come, desperate for it in a way that he can't explain.

Tolya doesn't make him wait long, thank fuck. "I— fuck—I'm gonna—he gasps—"

If anything, Mikey goes harder, determined to make him come. Within a few seconds Tolya rewards him with a sharp inhale, filling his mouth with the now-familiar taste of his release, shaking and shuddering above him as Mikey swallows again and again, dragging every last drop out of him.

"Stop, stop," Tolya finally gasps, urging him back

Mikey goes reluctantly, dragging the back of his hand

over his mouth. The sharp-edged need is still there, only a little sated by Tolya's release. He wants—he needs more.

"C'mere," Tolya mumbles, dragging at him with clumsy hands. Somehow, between the two of them, they manage to get Mikey to his feet.

He goes willingly when Tolya pulls him in for a kiss, even if it's softer, slower than he needs. "What do you want, Misha?" Tolya asks, brushing the hair out of his eyes.

For the second time since they entered the apartment, Mikey finds himself wordless, unable to answer. He shakes his head, frustrated arousal heating his cheeks, doing his best not to look too closely at the other emotions rising up.

Thankfully, Tolya seems to get it. "C'mon," he says, threading their fingers together. "Let's relocate this to a bed."

Mikey follows willingly, trying to ground himself in the physical. The squeeze of Tolya's fingers on his, the insistent throb of blood in his cock where it's tenting his sweatpants, the smell of sex in the air. This is real. This is happening.

His bedroom is closer, so it makes sense that Tolya leads them there, pushing through the door and not stopping until they're standing next to the bed. And it makes sense for Tolya to undress him—it goes much faster than if Mikey was taking off his clothes. Everything is very logical. And if the act of Tolya removing his clothes, the little grazes of skin on skin, the soft, intent expression in Tolya's eyes, makes him feel warm all over, well—

"I have an idea," Tolya says quietly. "If that's okay? If you don't like it, or you want something different, you can say—"

Mikey nods, the inconvenient lump still firmly lodged in his throat. Or maybe not so inconvenient; if it moves, if the flood of words and feelings trapped there starts pouring out—he forcibly drags his attention back to the present.

There's a lot to appreciate about the present. Tolya hooks his thumbs in the waistband of Mikey's sweats and boxers, pulling them slowly down to his feet. If he hadn't already been achingly hard, Tolya kneeling at his feet, looking up at him, would definitely get him there. As it is, his cock twitches visibly, as if to draw attention to itself.

Tolya laughs a little, smiling wider when Mikey joins in. "C'mon," he says, getting to his feet. "Can you, uh, sit on the bed? With your back to the headboard?"

Mikey wants to ask so many questions, but more than that, he wants to stop thinking, to find that mental space where it's just sensation. So he climbs clumsily onto the bed, situating himself with his back to the headboard.

He's just in time to watch Tolya shrugging out of his t-shirt, all those gorgeous muscles in his chest and arms and abs rippling and flexing with the movement. He'd apparently never bothered to button or zip his jeans back, Mikey notices absently, so peeling out of them is a quick process.

While he's bent over, pulling his feet free of jeans and socks, Mikey catches a quick flash of color, so fast he almost thinks he imagined it. "Is that—" He cuts off, the sound of his own voice surprising him.

Tolya shoots him a grin that looks almost shy, turning a little to give him a better view. And look, Mikey hasn't done that much with guys, but he knows enough to recognize the flat base of a butt plug, nestled between Tolya's cheeks.

"I thought—you've been feeling so much better, I figured we'd have something to celebrate," Tolya says, the words tumbling out so fast that Mikey has trouble separating them. "If you want."

Mikey nods, fast and jerky. "Can I—can I see?" he asks, barely forcing the words out, his throat gone tight again for completely different reasons.

"Yeah," Tolya says softly. His face is red as he climbs up onto the bed, turning a little awkwardly so Mikey can get a good look.

It's not that Mikey has spent a lot of time, or any time really, thinking about this. But now that it's happened, he's pretty sure this is going to be jerk-off material for like, the rest of his life. The way Tolya shivers when he runs his hand gently over the curve of his ass, the little noise he makes when Mikey's fingers brush the base of the plug, the stark contrast of the dark blue plastic against Tolya's paler skin, it's all so incredible, so overwhelming.

"We don't have to," Tolya says, breaking what Mikey

suddenly realizes is kind of a long silence. "If you don't want—"

"I want," Mikey says, biting his lip. "How do you—"

Tolya turns around to straddle Mikey's thighs. He looks gorgeous, the flush from his face spreading down his neck and across the top of his chest, his cock already half-hard again. "I was thinking, like this? I know you just got cleared for physio, but we should still be careful."

"Okay," Mikey agrees. He doesn't exactly have optimum blood flow to his brain, but that sounds—yeah. "C'mere?"

His hands are clumsy, of course—some day he'll remember not to try and use his right hand—but Tolya doesn't seem to care, settling into his lap and kissing him without hesitation, deep and wet and hungry. Like he's dying for the taste, like he hasn't just come a few minutes ago, like he wants nothing more than to kiss Mikey forever.

"Where's your lube?" he gasps when he finally pulls back, his hands digging into Mikey's shoulders for balance.

Mikey motions vaguely toward the bedside table, pressing a kiss to the corner of Tolya's jaw, then below his ear. He gets a little lost in the physical sensations, figuring out where lips or teeth or tongue will make Tolya shiver, or swear while he's trying to find the lube in the drawer.

When Tolya shifts back, he makes a vague noise of complaint, but then Tolya's hand wraps around the base of his cock, the cool latex of a condom rolling down the shaft. The groan he lets out when Tolya slicks him with lube is embarrassing, but it's nothing compared to the sound he makes when Tolya starts sinking slowly down on his cock.

"Fuck," Mikey chokes out, his good hand fisting in the sheets. Everything is Tolya; Tolya's hands braced on his shoulders, Tolya's teeth digging into his lower lip, most of all Tolya's body hot and tight around his cock. "Fuck, Tolya—"

"Yeah," Tolya gasps, finally meeting his eyes as he sinks down the last few centimeters, resting fully in Mikey's lap.

Mikey has no idea how long they stay like that, staring into each other's eyes, breathing each other's air, connected as intimately as two people can be. It feels like an eternity and, at the same time, like no time at all. A part of him wishes they could stay like this forever.

Finally, though, Tolya starts to move. Not a lot, just a slow, shallow grind, but enough to have Mikey throwing his head back against the headboard, his eyes doing their best to slide shut. "I'm close," he warns, clutching at Tolya's hip with his left hand, his almost-forgotten arousal rising up to claim all of his attention.

"Me, too," Tolya says breathlessly. His fingers flex on Mikey's shoulders, the tips digging in the same way that his teeth dig into his lower lip. "God, Misha—"

"I know," Mikey forces out. He feels like he can't get enough breath, his heart pounding in his chest, in his cock, in his fucking toes. "I know."

Tolya picks up speed, little bitten-off gasps and whimpers punching out of him with each stroke. It's all Mikey can do to hang on, to try and hold out long enough to make it good for both of them.

"Touch—me—" Tolya pants, never pausing his movements.

Mikey starts to reach, instinctively, with his right hand, only the weight of the cast reminding him at the last minute. *Fuck.* "I—my hand—"

"I don't—need—anything—fancy," Tolya bites out, and yeah, his fingers are probably going to leave bruises at this rate, the way he's holding onto Mikey's shoulders. That probably shouldn't be so hot. "Just—fucking —please—"

It feels clumsy, but Mikey manages to get his left hand around Tolya's cock, which earns him a truly spectacular noise. Thanks to Tolya's movements, really all he has to do is hold on, which he can manage. Barely.

Tolya doesn't seem to mind, though, his face intent as he chases his orgasm. Watching him—the way his body moves, the sheen of sweat over every rippling, flexing muscle, the flush that's spread down his face and across his chest—doesn't help Mikey at all in his quest to hold out. But he can't look away.

"I'm gonna—" Tolya pants, speeding up until he's practically slamming himself down onto Mikey's cock, hips rolling to thrust his cock into Mikey's hand. "Misha—"

"Yeah, come on," Mikey breathes, tightening his grip as best he can. "Come on me, Tolya—"

He watches in awe as Tolya does just that, his movements losing their purposeful rhythm as he comes, hot spurts streaking across Mikey's stomach. His whole body goes tight with his orgasm, reminding Mikey of his own half-forgotten arousal. He can't help fucking up into Tolya, just a little, and it feels so good that he does it again, and again.

A few thrusts later, Tolya's eyes flutter open, his ass clenching around Mikey's cock again, and that's it, that's all it takes for him to come, thrusting up as deep inside Tolya as he can get.

When he becomes aware of mundane things like his body again, he kind of never wants to move. The padded headboard is reasonably comfortable behind him—*good choice, past me*—and probably Tolya's weight slumped against him will get uncomfortable at some point, but for right now, it's good. Right.

Everything is good

Everything is terrible.

"Please?" Mikey asks, giving the physiotherapist— Amanda? No, wait, Ashley—his best puppy dog eyes.

"You're fine," she says mercilessly. "Give me ten more squats. You've got a broken arm, not a broken leg."

He groans. After weeks of enforced inactivity, not counting his impromptu living room spite workouts, his quads are burning, but he honestly doesn't mind as much as he's putting on. Even with the burn in his muscles, in his lungs, it feels good to be moving again. Familiar. Like getting back to normal.

"Watch your depth," Ashley says, eyeing him closely. "And don't forget to open your hips all the way at the top."

She's right, as much as he hates it. Shooting her a sarcastic salute, he focuses on making sure he drops all the way down as far as he can, until his hamstrings hit his calves. Of course, that means everything burns even more as he straightens up. But there's only eight left now. He can do anything eight times. Seven. Six. Five.

By the time he finishes the last rep, his legs are shaking and feel like they're made out of water, but he does it.

"Good." Ashley's approving smile doesn't falter when he drops heavily down to sit on the padded floor. "How are you feeling?"

"Like I'm never—standing up—again," he pants.

She shakes her head, smiling a little. "Any nausea? Headache?"

He takes a moment to check, taking stock of his body. And maybe it's the endorphins talking, but he can't find any problems. "Nope. All systems good."

"Your color's good," she says after studying his face for a moment. "But your hand look like it might swell up later. If it does, take some ibuprofen. No more exercise today; stick to it and I'll clear you for skating tomorrow."

"Really?" Mikey asks.

She nods. "You're not going to be able to practice until the cast comes off, but there's no reason you can't be on the ice. If—" she fixes him with an intimidating stare—"you take it easy for the rest of the day."

"Wait a second," Mikey says as something occurs to him. "How are we defining 'taking it easy?'"

"No more strenuous exercise," Ashley says, narrowing her eyes at him. "So, for example, no going from here to the arena and doing another workout."

His face heats as he tries to think of a way to dance around the subject and still get an answer. "Okay but, like, what about things that, uh, aren't technically exercise?"

"Things—" Ashley's face does something interesting when she finally gets what he's talking about. The corners of her mouth twitch a little bit, but otherwise she manages not to smile. "As long as these other things aren't especially, ah, athletic, I think you'll probably be okay. If you promise to stop if you start feeling bad, or hurting anywhere. Deal?"

He offers her a pinky and after a second she hooks hers round it. "Deal," he says, letting her take his hand and pull him to his feet.

"Good," she says, letting go once he's steady. "See you next week."

Mikey's good mood can't be touched by the wobbly feeling in his legs as he walks out to the waiting area. Just the thought of getting to be on the ice again is incredible. He hasn't gone this long without skating since—maybe not ever, he realizes.

Tolya stands up from the waiting room chair as soon as Mikey pushes through the door from the back area, shoving his phone into his pocket. "Judging from the smile on your face, I guess it went well."

"I mean, my legs feel like I'm going to fall on my ass at any moment," Mikey says. "But Ashley says I can skate on Friday!"

"Really?" Tolya's matching smile blooms slowly across his face. "Misha, that's awesome!"

He accepts Tolya's congratulatory hug, even if he is smelly and covered in sweat—hell, Tolya's been just as close to him when he was covered in worse things. Closer, even. "But no more workouts today. So I can ride along with you to practice, but I'll probably just hang out in the trainers room."

"For sure," Tolya agrees, helping him on with his coat before they head out the door.

It's nothing he hasn't done dozens of times since Mikey's injury, but for some reason it makes Mikey feel kind of guilty. Like, sure, Tolya likes taking care of people; it makes him happy. But even so, he's been doing a lot for Mikey, and not getting anything back, really. That's just as bullshit as if he was jerking Mikey off without any reciprocation. Tolya deserves better.

Tolya deserves so much better.

Only about half of his attention is on their conversation as Tolya drives them to the arena; the other half is busy coming up with an excellent plan. It's not like Mikey's keeping score or anything, which is good. Because if he was, there's no way even his excellent plan would come close to evening things out.

But hopefully it'll let Tolya know that Mikey doesn't take him for granted. That Mikey appreciates him being there, like he always is.

Ignoring the sinking feeling in his stomach, the little voice asking what he'll do someday when Tolya isn't there, Mikey starts to put his plan into action

Two days after moving in

"We need to get more Gatorade," Mikey says, suddenly realizing as they drive home from the arena. "We're out."

"No we aren't," Tolly replies calmly, driving right past the turn they need.

Mikey rolls his eyes. "I drank the last one yesterday, dude. We're out."

"I ordered grocery delivery last night," Tolly says. "We were almost out of bread and Clif bars, too. The delivery probably got there while we were at practice."

"Um." Mikey blinks at him for a moment. "Dude, how are you this good at adulating?"

Tolly makes a scoffing noise. "Living on my own for the last three years in the minors."

"Well, I'm glad one of us is good at it," Mikey says.

They drive closer to their building, music from the radio barely audible over the sound of their tires on the road.

"Oh, and I got more mangoes," Tolly says. "Since you like them."

"Wow," Mikey says, trying not to show his surprise. "You're like, really good at this."

Tolly jerks one shoulder in a half-assed shrug, his ears going pink. "I like it. Remembering what people like and stuff. It makes me happy."

"Well, if it means I get mangoes and don't have to remember to buy Gatorade, then count me in."

When they get home, they're greeted by a neat row of grocery bags lined up on the kitchen counter, which prove to hold not only mangoes and Gatorade, but a small container of Smarties. Tolly blushes a darker pink when he sees Mikey holding them.

"You said they were your favorite."

"I can't believe you remembered that," Mikey says.

Tolly ducks his head. "Like I said, it makes me happy."

Mikey wants to push, to ask more, but the thought of having a conversation about what his mom calls "love languages" with his new roomie and d-partner is just too uncomfortable. "Okay," he says.

"Okay," Tolly replies, his shoulders relaxing back down from his ears as he puts the Gatorade in the fridge.

13

———

TOLYA

"Good practice?" Misha asks when Tolya finally finds him hanging out in the trainers room, chatting with Sara the massage therapist and Malik the strength coach.

"Yeah," Tolya says, because it was. Nothing too fancy, and he still sometimes catches himself looking over at empty ice instead of Misha, but it was a good, solid practice. His muscles ache in the slightly used way that tells him he worked hard. "Ready to head out, get some food?"

Misha nods, waving goodbye to Sara and Malik. "Yeah, I've got dinner taken care of."

Maybe it's because Tolya's tired, but it takes a few moments for the words to make sense. "You're not cooking, are you?" he asks, regretting the harshness of the words as soon as they're out of his mouth. But honestly, the thought of Misha attempting to cook—he remembers the abortive attempts at warming things up in the microwave and resigns himself to an evening spent cleaning the kitchen, barely suppressing a shudder.

"No, asshole," Misha laughs, practically vibrating with excitement and clearly not offended. He must be really pumped about getting to skate again tomorrow. "I ordered delivery. It's a surprise. But we need to get moving so the food isn't like, getting cold while we're stuck in traffic."

"Okay," Tolya says, relaxing and allowing himself to be steered toward the parkade. "Let's go home, then. I hope whatever you ordered is on my diet plan so I don't get in trouble with Susan."

Misha rolls his eyes. "Susan said you're fine for a couple of cheat days a week, and you haven't had one yet this week. Don't worry about it."

"You're really not going to tell me?" Tolya asks, slightly bemused as they pass through the door to the parkade and head toward where they left his car.

"Nope," Misha answers, his smug voice echoing off the concrete around them.

They arrive at the car before Misha can notice his disbelief, which is probably a good thing. As they're settling in and buckling their seat belts, Tolya places a mental bet with himself as to how long Misha can actually keep from ruining his own surprise, then revises it when he notices that Misha's knee is jittering up and down with excitement.

Much to his surprise, despite a near-constant stream of

chatter, Misha doesn't let any information slip on the drive. Not even when Tolya makes leading comments like "been awhile since we had poutine, eh?" or "man, that one taco place was so delicious, didn't you say it tasted just like your mom's recipe?"

Misha just agrees mildly, smiling back at him.

Finally they manage to navigate to their parking stalls and make their way up the elevator to the apartment. He should probably find Misha's visible excitement annoying, but it's too cute. Yet another sign that he's in deep here.

"Go on," Misha says, shooing him toward his room. "Get changed. I'll take care of stuff out here."

"Want me to slip into something more comfortable?" Tolya teases with an exaggerated eyebrow waggle.

Misha raises him a slow, obvious up-and-down look that leaves him feeling almost naked and very tempted just to forget dinner and haul him off to the bedroom. "Yeah, get comfy. Food should be here any minute. I've got this."

"Okay," Tolya says, bemused.

He keeps an ear out while he's changing, of course. It's practically second nature by now, always listening for the subtle signs that Misha needs him. It's hard to believe that soon he won't have to, that Misha will be perfectly fine on his own. Maybe even in another city, with another team—

Forcibly pushing that thought aside, Tolya pulls on his favorite worn-soft sweatpants and t-shirt, which is technically Misha's, from when they accidentally switched shirts at training camp and didn't realize until the end of the day. Doing his best not to think too hard about why it feels so right to have Misha's name resting between his shoulderblades, he opens his door and heads back into the living area.

He arrives just in time to hear a knock on the door, which Misha promptly opens. "Thanks, Ruth," he says, taking a couple of paper bags from the building concierge and handing her some folded bills. "I appreciate it."

"No problem," she answers, her smile white against her dark skin. "How's your arm doing?"

"Oh, you know," Misha says with a shrug. "Good days and bad days."

She nods, stepping back. "Well, we're looking forward to seeing you back on the ice soon. Enjoy your dinner!"

"Will do," Misha says, shutting the door gently and turning to carry the bags to the bar.

"Do you think she's gonna sell information about your arm to the Werewolves or something?" Tolya asks, amused.

Misha shakes his head, his face flushing as he rounds the bar to find plates. "Nah, but you know me. I like to talk. I'd rather be a little vague with Ruth than have the front office put me through yet another seminar about when to have someone sign an NDA."

"Fair," Tolya concedes.

He heads for the kitchen to help, but Misha waves him off. "No, I've got this. I'm a little slow, but I've got it. Go sit on the couch; I'll be there in a minute."

Despite his better judgment, and the familiar smells of meat and grease that are slowly wafting toward him, Tolya does as he's told, settling into his favorite corner of the couch. He's distracted, which is why it takes a minute for him to realize that *Captain America: The Winter Soldier* is queued up on the TV.

"What—" he asks, turning to look at Misha. Who is, it turns out, just then rounding the end of the couch with a plate holding a burger and a pile of fries.

"You've been taking care of me for weeks," Misha says simply, handing him the plate. "I figured it was my turn."

Smiling softly, he heads back into the kitchen, leaving Tolya staring dumbly at the plate. At his favorite comfort-slash-guilty pleasure food, at his favorite superhero movie ready to watch. At the beer—his favorite craft brand, but at least that was already in the fridge—that Misha hands him, setting a Gatorade for himself on the coffee table before going back one more time for his own food.

"You don't have to—" he starts to say when Misha is finally settled in with a plate of greasy goodness.

"I know," Misha says, quiet but firm. "I wanted to."

Tolya doesn't really know what to do with that information, or the warm glow in his chest. He reaches for the remote to start the movie before he remembers. "You've already used some of your screen time for today, so you can't watch the whole movie."

Gesturing to his mouth, Misha chews and swallows the food in his mouth before speaking. "Yeah, but I can watch for a little while, then I can listen to the rest. And you can tell me what's going on in case I forget. Which I won't, because we've watched this movie at least six times since September, because you're a giant fucking nerd."

"Hey," Tolya objects mildly. "First of all, I'm not the one who knows all the words to every Disney song ever made."

"Two words. Little. Sisters."

Tolya rolls his eyes. "I've heard you singing *Let It Go* in the shower, don't even pretend. Secondly, Disney owns the Marvel movies, so Steve Rogers and Bucky Barnes are Disney princes."

Misha picks up a fry, examining it closely. "You're not presenting any evidence for not being a giant fucking nerd here."

"Anyway, liking Marvel movies isn't nerdy. It's mainstream now," Tolya argues. He can't help grinning even though he knows he doesn't have a leg to stand on here. This easy back and forth is the kind of fun they haven't really had much chance for lately. It feels good.

"Maybe," Misha leans heavily on the word, "liking them isn't nerdy. But your mom sent me pictures of your comic collection. And pictures of the last time you dressed up to go to a convention. Ergo, you're a giant fucking nerd."

Tolya presses his lips together, trying to hide his smile. It's not really working, but that's okay. Misha's smiling, too. "Fine. But you watched it all six times and you're about to settle in for number seven. If I'm a nerd, so are you."

"Maybe I'm just a good friend," Misha retorts, his eyes sparkling.

"You are, you know," Tolya says softly as he hits the play button. "The best friend."

He can't meet Misha's eyes, at least not until Misha's good hand covers his, squeezing gently. "You are, too," Misha says, his voice just as soft.

And then the movie starts, Steve Rogers and Sam Wilson running and bantering around the National Mall. The conversation turns to less fraught topics, like if Steve and Sam were flirting—they totally were—and Tolya can forget, just for a little while, that this all might be coming to an end any day now.

ANDREA'S TEXT pops up on his phone while Misha is still napping, so Tolya is able to let her and Diana into the apartment quietly.

"Hey," he says, taking their bags. "How was the drive?"

Diana rolls her eyes at her twin, looking so much like Misha for a moment that Tolya can't believe it. "This one drives like a maniac. I can't believe Mom and Dad let her get her license."

"We're not dead yet," Andrea retorts, but more quietly than usual. "Anyway, why waste time on the road when we could be doing other things?"

"If we crash and die, we won't get to do anything," Diana says wearily. "Ever."

If Tolya hadn't heard some variation of this same argument every time he'd interacted with Misha's sisters, he'd be worried. As it is, he takes his cue from how Misha and their parents handle it and opts to ignore it.

"Are you hungry?" he asks, heading toward his room to drop off their bags. "Help yourself to anything in the fridge, except the beer."

"Awww, you're no fun," Andrea pouts behind him. "Our birthday's next month, you know."

Tolya doesn't bother to respond to that, setting their bags just inside his bedroom door. Leaving it open, he returns to the living area. "Yes, and you'll be seventeen on your birthday," he says in answer to Andrea's pleading eyes. "Which is still a whole year from being legal to drink. Besides, you're here to make sure M—Mikey doesn't do anything stupid. How are you gonna do that if you're drunk?"

"Fine, bring logic into it," Andrea sighs, flopping onto the couch. "Is the wifi password still the same?"

"Yeah," Tolya says. "And the TV remotes are right there. I need to finish packing, but let me know if you can't find anything."

They wave him off in unison as Diana joins her twin on the couch, already bickering over what to watch. Tolya shakes his head and goes back to shove the last toiletries into his shaving bag, and to double-check that he hasn't left anything incriminating out where inquisitive teenage girls might find it. He changed the sheets first thing this morning, relocated the condoms and lube and everything else from his bedside drawer to Misha's room, much to Misha's amusement.

He can't find anything else, no matter how he wracks his brain. There's almost certainly something he's forgetting, but he resigned himself to teenage girl chirps months ago, ever since the first time he met Misha's family and they folded him in like another part of them, accepting without question.

There's no more stalling then. He hauls his bags out to the living room, hesitating behind the couch where both girls are apparently ignoring some sort of reality show in favor of whatever's on their phone screens—some kind of game for Andrea, texting for Diana, her fingers flying over the screen.

"So," he says a little awkwardly. "I have to head out for the airport. Make sure he doesn't do anything dumb while I'm gone?"

"Dumb, or dumber than usual?" Andrea asks, not bothering to look up from her game.

Diana shakes her head, actually looking up at him. "Don't worry, Tolly. If he gets stubborn, we'll call Mom."

"Okay," Tolya says. Realistically, he knows Misha's in good hands. He's been recovering well, he's got his sisters to keep him company, He probably won't even notice Tolya's gone. "I don't want to wake him up. Just tell him I said—"

He goes blank. What can he even say? Especially filtered through Misha's sisters.

"Tell him I said not to do anything stupid until I get back," he finishes, falling back on movie references.

From the way both twins smirk at him, he's pretty sure they caught that, and also the underlying context. Oh well.

"Will do," Andrea promises. "Go kick some Kraken ass!"

Tolya tosses her an ironic little salute, hauling his bags out the door and waiting for the click of it locking behind him before he makes is way to the elevator.

And then he spends the whole elevator ride to the parkade trying to convince himself that he's not worried.

Yes, this roadie is going to last an entire week, but Misha's doing much better. Even though he overdid it at the gym the other day, Tolya's pretty sure the lecture he got from Sara and Malik and all of the coaches is enough to convince him to pay better attention. And he's got Diana and Andrea there in case he needs help and isn't able to call, even if his mom had tried to make it seem like a "your sisters finished their finals early, please let them come stay with you, they're driving me crazy" visit.

He's going to be fine.

Maybe if Tolya keeps repeating that to himself, he'll actually believe it.

"Hey," Misha says when the call connects, his voice soft and low. "You left without saying goodbye."

"I didn't want to wake you," Tolya replies, automatically lowering his voice as well and settling back against the pillows of his hotel bed. "You need rest to get better."

Misha scoffs. "I wanted to give you a goodbye kiss. For luck."

The idea has something warm and aching settling in Tolya's chest. "Next time," he promises, hoping that circumstances don't make him a liar. "Are you in bed?"

"Yeah," Misha says, his voice cracking on a yawn. "The twins bossed me into bed fifteen minutes ago. But I was waiting for you to call. Gotta have my story to fall asleep, since you're not here to fuck me."

Tolya's cock is half-hard so fast he's a little dizzy with it. "You can't just say shit like that," he splutters, trying to keep his voice low, since Sunshine is on the other side of the wall. Hotels are not known for being soundproof.

Misha's voice is quiet, too. Not that he needs to be, since their bedrooms are on opposite ends of the apartment and there's no way his sisters could hear him unless he yelled. But it makes Tolya feel a little better about what they're doing here. "I can say whatever I want," he retorts.

"Are you really trying to have phone sex?" Tolya asks incredulously. "Mr. I-can't-even-jerk-off-anymore? How do you see this working out?"

"Well," Misha says slowly, drawing the word out. "I was thinking I could get out that dildo in my drawer and you could tell me what to do with it. See if that works better than trying it on my own."

Tolya swallows hard, the rest of the blood in his brain

rushing to vacate it and fill his stupid, aching cock. "Take it into your bathroom," he orders. "Unless you want the twins busting in on you because they think you're hurt again. And don't forget the lube."

"Yes, sir," Misha says half-mockingly.

Tolya can hear the rustling of his sheets, the soft slap of his feet on the hardwood floor, the sound of the door closing behind him as he, presumably, went into the bathroom. But not, he realizes, the sound of the bedside drawer opening and closing. "Misha?" he asks hoarsely. "Did you already have the dildo and the lube out?"

"I was hopeful," Misha admits. The quality of the sound changes, becomes more tinny as he puts the phone on speaker. "What should I do first?"

"What would you want me to do?" Tolya asks, turning the question around on him. "If I was there with you."

He hums softly, the sound almost a sigh. "I'd want you to kiss me, first," Misha admits.

Tolya's chest hurts with how much he wants that, how much he wishes he was there to do it. "Pretend I am," he says instead, doing his best to picture it. "Close your eyes, pretend I'm there, kissing you just like you want. Are you naked?"

"Boxers," Misha says, soft and almost shy.

"That's good," Tolya replies, doing his best to push everything he's feeling, everything he wants, into his voice. "Touch yourself first, all over your chest and down your stomach, like I'm there to touch you."

The noise that comes through the phone into his ear is

somewhere between a gasp and a moan. If he hadn't already been hard and aching, tenting the soft cotton of his boxers, that noise would have been enough to get him there. Misha sounds fucking wrecked, and Tolya isn't even touching him. Just lying there, listening to Misha breathe his name from hundreds of miles away.

"Tolya," he gasps again. "Please—"

"What do you want, Misha?" Tolya asks, doing his best to keep his voice gentle. "What do you need?"

If he closes his eyes, he can picture it. Misha standing in his bathroom, his one good hand moving over his body, cock hard in his boxers. "Off," he gasps. "Please, Tolya, let me take them off."

"Yeah, do it," Tolya says, lifting his hips to slide his own underwear off and kicking them onto the floor. "Are you hard?"

"Y-yeah." Misha trips over the word, like he does sometimes when he's very turned on. "Are—are you?"

"I've been hard since you told me what you wanted to do," Tolya tells him. "Next time I want to be there. I want to watch."

An indrawn breath. "I could send you snaps?" Misha suggests, his voice tentative.

Tolya opens his mouth to agree, then realizes he's being stupid. "Hang on," he says, fumbling with his phone. "I'm gonna call you right back."

He barely waits for Misha's affirmative reply before hanging up and opening the Signal app. It only takes a few seconds for the video call to connect, and then he gets to see Misha's face, flushed almost as red as his lower lip where his teeth are digging in.

"Why didn't I think of this?" Misha asks.

"It took me a minute," Tolya reminds him. "We could waste time talking about it, or you could show me what you're doing."

Misha swallows, his throat working. "Right. Uh, what should I do?"

"Let me see the dildo," Tolya says, trying his best to stay focused, to make it good for Misha.

Biting his lip harder, Misha sets the phone down on something—probably the bathroom counter, from the height, and holds up a translucent purple dildo. From the look of it, it's a little longer than Tolya's cock, but thinner, which is probably better for their purposes. And there's a suction cup on the base.

Tolya can feel his smile stretching across his face as the plan comes together in his mind. "Does that suction cup work?"

"I've never tried," Misha admits, his face going even redder.

"See if it'll stick on that corner of the tub," Tolya suggests.

It does stick, as it turns out, standing purple and proud against the white of the tub. And as a bonus, Tolya gets to watch Misha climbing in and bending over to secure it.

"Okay, now what?" Misha asks, coming back toward the camera.

"Get some lube on your fingers," Tolya directs, doing his best to ignore the drumbeat of arousal in his cock. "Go ahead and take it with you. Get one knee up on the side of the tub so I can see what you're doing."

He didn't think it was possible for Misha to get redder but, as it turns out, he was wrong. "Oh, God," Misha says faintly as he turns to obey.

"Is this okay?" Tolya asks. It's hot—good God, it's hot, seeing Misha back and ass ripple as he settles himself, bracing his casted arm and knee on the side of the tub. "We can stop if you need—"

"Fuck, no," Misha interrupts, reaching behind himself. "I just—it's a lot, you know?"

Tolya nods, even though Misha isn't watching the phone, can't see him. "I know. You look so good, though."

He watches in awe as the flush travels down Misha's upper back, but then his attention is stolen by Misha's hand, coming back to slide down into the cleft of his ass.

Tolya wants to be there, to be closer. Close enough to feel the heat coming off Misha's skin, to hear more clearly the little gasps and feel the shivers as he presses a finger inside.

"Slow down," he says, fisting his free hand in the sheets to keep from touching himself, from ending this too soon. "It's not a race."

"I want—" Misha pants, his hips jerking a little, but he does slow down. "I'm still a little, uh, loose. From last time."

Swallowing at the memory of "last time," Misha riding

him slow and lazy on the couch, his eyes wide and dark, Tolya watches intently. There's no sign of discomfort in Misha's body, though, just the loose, almost liquid movements as he tries out different movements, different angles. "How does it feel?" he asks hoarsely.

Misha shrugs one shoulder. "It feels okay," he says, pulling his hand out and reaching for the lube again. "I want another one. I think that's all I need."

"Two is probably enough," Tolya agrees, his eyes glued to the tiny screen as the two fingers sink slowly inside Misha's body. "What about now? How does it feel?"

"It's not enough," Misha says, his voice tight with arousal and frustration. "I can't—I can't reach? I don't know. Wish you were here."

And that—yeah. That's all Tolya wants, in this moment. "Me, too," he says softly. "You're doing so good. What do you think? Are you ready?"

"I—yeah. I'm ready," Misha says, pulling his fingers slowly free.

"Get that dildo good and wet," Tolya orders. He bites his lip when Misha obeys, carefully slicking the dildo until every inch of it is glistening with lube. "Okay, turn around and sit down on it. Slowly. Be careful."

He has to swallow back a noise when Misha turns around. His cock is still hard, the foreskin pulled back under the head, the skin shiny with precome. It bobs in midair as Misha reaches behind himself again. Tolya can just barely see, between Misha's spread legs, the way his hand wraps around the dildo, holding it in position.

And then he starts to sink down. Slowly, so slowly. Tolya doesn't realize he's holding his breath at first, until his lungs start to burn with it. He's too focused on Misha's face, the way his eyes flutter closed as he starts to lower himself, the slight tremor in his leg muscles as he controls his descent.

"Talk to me, Mishenka," Tolya says, nearly pleads. "How does it feel?"

"Different," Misha says faintly, moving down another few centimeters. "Not bad, but—it's not you."

Probably Tolya shouldn't be so happy that he compares favorably with an inanimate hunk of silicone, but whatever. "Does it hurt?" he asks, finally allowing himself one long, slow stroke over his cock, shuddering a little when his fist closes around the head.

"No," Misha sighs, panting slightly as he comes to rest on the side of the tub. "No, it doesn't—it doesn't hurt."

"Good," Tolya says. "Take your time. When you feel ready, I want to watch you fuck yourself on it."

Misha's lips, wet and red, fall open as he draws a breath. "Oh, God," he says again.

Even with most of the blood gone from his brain, Tolya can put two and two together. Especially since this isn't exactly a huge leap. "You like me telling you what to do?" he asks softly.

"Yeah," Misha says, so quietly he almost can't hear it, has to read it in the shape of his mouth. "God, Tolya, please—"

"You look so good," Tolya says. It's strangely easy, just

letting his mouth run, letting everything he's thinking go free instead of holding it in. He would've expected to be more embarrassed but—it's Misha. Everything is easier with Misha. "Can't wait to watch you fuck yourself on it, just like last time. You felt so good, riding me on the couch. Hot and slick and tight around my cock—"

Misha makes a whimpering sound, lifts up just slightly and drops it back down. Then again, more. "Oh, fuck," he breathes, the shudder rolling through his whole body. "Oh, fuck, Tolya—"

"Yeah, just like that," Tolya says, stroking his hand over his cock before he even realizes he's moved. "Slow and steady. Can you touch your cock for me, baby?"

"Oh, fuck," Misha says again, but he does it, curling his left hand clumsily around his cock. "I can't—"

"I know," Tolya says. "I know that's not enough. Just leave it there, okay? Leave it there while you fuck yourself on that dildo for me."

Misha's chest heaves with his breath as he complies, rising and falling further every time.

"That's it, baby." Tolya's eyes are glued to the screen, hungry for every detail. "Pretend I'm there, and you're riding me, just like last time—"

He cuts off at the soft, punched-out noise Misha makes. "Oh—oh fuck—fuck," he pants, his body writhing as he fucks himself down on the dildo, hard and fast. He's not hitting his prostate every time, Tolya can tell, but it's still enough to have him obviously on the edge of orgasm.

"That's it, baby," Tolya says, speeding up his strokes.

"Come on, Misha, come for me. I want to see you, let me see you, baby, please—"

Misha comes with a soft cry, his body arching back as he slams down onto the dildo one last time. It only takes a couple of strokes, a couple of moments looking at him, messy and debauched and gorgeous, before Tolya comes, too, rolling over to muffle his groan into the pillow.

When he pries his eyes open again, Misha is looking back at him from the screen, smug and self-satisfied. "I'll take my bedtime story now," he says with a shit-eating grin.

First weekend after moving in

"Oh, shit," Mikey says faintly, sitting bolt upright on the bar stool they had delivered yesterday.

"What's up?" Tolya asks, looking up from his phone.

Mikey meets his eyes, looking panicky. "Look, we don't have a lot of time. I just need you to promise me that no matter what they say or do, we're going to be okay."

"Slow down," Tolya says. "What the fuck are you talking about?"

"So, uh, my family drove up for a surprise visit. Mom just texted me. They're downstairs right now."

Tolya can't help but laugh. "That's all? I thought maybe somebody died or something."

Mikey's expression doesn't change. "Look, my parents are

great. Mom raised me on her own for like four years before she married Dad. But they brought the twins."

"Your sisters, right?" Tolya is pretty sure he remembers this from one of their earlier conversations.

"Andrea and Diana." Mikey pronounces the names like he's naming Horsemen of the Apocalypse. "They're sixteen and they think they know everything. You'll see."

Tolya shakes his head. "It's fine. I have teenage cousins."

Mikey slides off his barstool, heading for his room. "I better get pants on. They're on the way up."

Sure enough, someone knocks on their door just as Mikey re-emerges, basketball shorts pulled on over his boxers. He gives Tolya one last martyred look before crossing to the door and unlocking the deadbolt.

"Kevin!" The chorus of voices is startlingly loud, and also just startling until Tolya remembers that Mikey has an actual, legal first name.

Mikey doesn't quite stagger backward under the impact, but he does sway slightly on his feet when three bodies wrap themselves around him in one massive hug. All three women are shorter than Mikey, short enough that Tolya can see over their heads to the red-haired man behind them, closing the door and smiling fondly at them.

"Let me look at you, mijo," *a woman who must be Mikey's mom commands, pulling back far enough to take his face in her hands. "Are you eating enough?"*

"Yes, mom," Mikey says, his tone long-suffering, but he smiles back at her. "Trust me, they're making sure I do. And Tolly is like, a kung fu master of grocery shopping."

His mom clicks her tongue skeptically, but she turns toward Tolly, holding out her hands. "Excuse our manners. I'm Erika, Kevin's mom."

"Tolya," he says, letting her take his hands. He hasn't lived at home since before Juniors, but he's suddenly hit by a wave of homesickness. "Well, Anatoly, but—"

She nods like she gets it. "Tolya, then. These hooligans pretending to be teenage girls are my daughters, Andrea and Diana. And my husband, Brent."

"Nice to meet you, son," Brent says, shaking Tolya's offered hand. "We've heard a lot about you from Kevin."

"Yeah, we have," one of the identical girls says, eyeing him up and down like she can see everything wrong with him and isn't sure how she feels about it.

Mikey's mom shakes her head. "Andrea," she says resignedly. "We're guests."

Andrea rolls her eyes. "So he gets a CHL contract and suddenly you don't care who he's friends with?"

"How about breakfast?" Mikey says hurriedly. "There's a really great brunch place a couple of blocks away. My treat."

"That sounds lovely, mijo*," Mikey's mom says warmly. "We'll just use the restroom first and then we can go. It's a long drive from Calgary."*

Mikey shows his mom the powder room and directs Andrea to his ensuite. Tolya does the same for the as-yet-silent Diana, trying frantically to remember if he'd left anything embarrassing out in plain view.

"Tell me about your practices," Brent says to Mikey,

shooting Tolya a sympathetic smile. "How are you feeling? What do they want you to work on?"

Mikey launches into a detailed catalogue of training camp and their practices since then, with Tolya making the occasional interjection, and before he knows it, Erika and the twins are back and they're all heading out the door.

Tolya has just started to relax, leaning against the elevator wall and listening to the way Mikey talks to his family, when Diana turns to him and says, abruptly, "Falcon is clearly a better superhero than Captain America."

He's still blinking at her when he catches Mikey's sympathetic look over her head, sees him mouth "I'm sorry."

"First of all," Diana says, clearly tired of waiting for a verbal response, "Falcon received actual military tactical training…"

It's not until later that evening that Tolya realizes what that debate meant, even though he'd lost soundly by any manner. When Erika hugs him after dinner, too, and tells him, "Take good care of my Kevin, okay mijo?" *not waiting for a response before she hugs Mikey too and sweeps her husband and daughters up in her wake and out the door.*

"Congratulations," Mikey says dryly, dropping down onto the couch. "You've been adopted.

"I think I'm okay with that," Tolya says slowly.

Mikey grins at him. "Cool."

14

"What's up?" Andrea asks.

"Huh?" Mikey looks over at her, curled up in the corner of the couch. "Nothing."

She eyes him narrowly, looking so much like his mom that he has to suppress the urge to confess any number of stupid things. "Right," she says, drawing the word out like only a teenage girl can.

Diana joins in from his other side, making him feel like he's caught in an echo chamber of judgement.

"No, seriously," he says, only stopped from crossing his arms over his chest by the cast. "What the f—heck are you talking about?"

Andrea rolls her eyes. "First of all, I'm sixteen, I've heard the word 'fuck' before. We both have. And second, you've been moping around like someone just killed your dog."

"I don't have a dog," Mikey retorts.

"No shit, Sherlock," Diana sighs. "The point, dumbass, is that Tolly said you were doing good, getting better. And then we show up and you spend the whole time looking pathetic."

Mikey rubs his good hand over his face. They're his sisters, and he loves them. And they love him. But damn, he'd forgotten how annoying they could be sometimes.

"I am," he says. "Doing better, I mean. But everyone's talking about these trade rumors—"

"That's bullshit," Andrea says, scowling ferociously. "They're not gonna trade you."

He shrugs. "They might. Or they might just send me down to the farm team. That's the game. No point in having me here using up cap space when I can't even play."

"First of all, like Andi said, that's bullshit," Diana puts in. "Second, that's not the only thing bugging you. Spill."

"You're not the boss of me," Mikey mutters, doing his best to hold all his stupid emotions behind his teeth instead of word-vomiting them onto his teenage sisters. "I'm five years older than you."

Andrea's eyes gleam with a familiar, terrifying light. "Talk, Kevin. Or we'll have to pull out the big guns."

"What, you'll call Mom?" he scoffs.

Diana laughs. "Oh, buddy. No, no. We have ways of making you talk."

That's the only warning he gets before they converge

on him, their fingers mercilessly finding the ticklish spots in his ribs. There's no escape—they have him boxed in from both sides. It only takes a few minutes of helpless giggling before he yells "Uncle! Uncle!!! I give, I give."

They retreat, but not far, still clearly a threat. "Talk," Diana says.

"It's Tolya—Tolly," he says reluctantly, wincing a little when they exchange a look at his slip of the tongue. "We play really well together—he makes me better. If I get traded, or sent down, I might not ever be good enough to come back."

Andrea raises a skeptical eyebrow. "And that's the only reason? How well you play together?"

Mikey rolls his eyes. "No, obviously. He's my friend, he's a great roommate—"

"You have a giant crush on him," Diana interjects.

"I do not!" Mikey retorts automatically.

The skepticism intensifies so much he can practically feel it in the air. "You practically have heart eyes whenever you talk about him," Andrea says. "Come on, you can tell us."

"He's a really good friend," Mikey says, unable to keep the defensive edge out of his voice. "He's taken care of me this whole time. He's a great guy!"

"No arguments here," Diana says. "And also you have a giant crush on him."

Mikey lets his head fall back against hte back of the couch. "I wouldn't say it's a crush—"

"What would you say it is?" Andrea asks instantly.

"I don't even know," Mikey admits, closing his eyes. "I mean, he's my friend, but also, like, have you seen him?"

A pause, where he can practically hear the twins exchanging looks over his head. "Yeah, he's pretty cute for an older guy," Diana says.

Mikey opens his mouth to take issue with the "older guy" comment, but some things just aren't worth it. Also, Tolya is older than them, so they're not wrong "And, you know, it's not just taking care of me here? He thinks of things. Like, all the dog photos on my Insta since I got hurt? He took them for me on his run, because I couldn't."

"Really?" Andrea asks. "All he has on his Insta is gym selfies and pictures of his gross healthy food."

"Really. Even when I couldn't look at the phone screen, he'd tell me about them—shit. Can we talk about something else?" he asks plaintively.

"Yeah, okay," Andrea says, her voice gentle. "Wanna watch Frozen?"

"Kind of," he says, eyes still closed. "But only if you sing the songs with me."

Diana sighs, shifting closer to him. "Fine, but if you every tell anyone about this, you're dead."

"And we might just bring you back so we can kill you again," Andrea agrees.

Mikey leans over to kiss the top of her head, then Andrea's when she snuggles into his other side. "Got it."

HE'S IN THE KITCHEN, surveying the nearly-empty shelves in the refrigerator and wondering how two teenage girls can eat so much, when the apartment door opens. "Honey, I'm home," Tolya calls, nudging the door closed behind himself.

"How was your day, dear?" Mikey asks in as ridiculous a falsetto as he can manage, closing the fridge and doing his best to ignore the raised-eyebrow looks he's getting from the twins.

"Fucking long," Tolya grumbles, hauling his bags toward his room.

"Oh, no, I'm a CHL player and I have to fly on a private plane with specially catered meals," Andrea says sarcastically. "We should start a special charity for you."

Tolya sticks his tongue out at her. "Yeah, yeah. I was going to take you out to dinner, but maybe you two should just stay here."

Mikey watches the girls exchange looks with a feeling of impending doom. "Actually," Diana says, "since you're back, we were going to try and catch up with one of our friends who moved to Edmonton a few years ago. Do you remember Daria, Kevin?"

"I think so," he says slowly. "She lives here now?"

"Yeah," Andrea says. "Her dad got a job here so they had to move. We talk online, but she said she wanted to meet up if we had time while we were here. Apparently there's an all-ages concert tonight, so we were gonna get together with her for food and then go to the concert."

He eyes them suspiciously. "Why didn't you say anything before?"

"We didn't want you to feel guilty if Tolly got delayed and we couldn't go." Diana's face is a picture of innocent sisterly devotion.

"I'm not an invalid," he says, aware he's taking the bait but unable to help himself. "You could've gone even if Tol—Tolly didn't make it back."

Andrea nods. "Oh, yeah, for sure. But he's back, so it's all good. We'll get changed and head out, and you two can have a nice dinner, get all caught up without us there to bug you."

"Fine," Mikey finally says. "But you text me the address for every place you go, and if you're not back by one I'm calling the police. Got it?"

"Deal," they say in unison, popping up off the couch and heading for Tolya's room, presumably to change clothes.

Mikey and Tolya are left staring at each other, the slightly shell-shocked look on Tolya's face matching the way Mikey feels.

"Are they always like this?" Tolya asks a little plaintively, leaving his bags by the door and crossing to the couch. "I can't remember."

"Sometimes they're worse," Mikey says, joining him. He maybe leans a little closer than he was planning, but then Tolya slides an arm around his shoulder, pulling him close. And yeah, that's exactly where he wanted to be, the last of the unsettled feeling sliding away. "You said something about dinner?"

Tolya nods, his hand squeezing Mikey's arm. "Yeah, in a minute. Right now it's just good to be home, you know?"

"Yeah," Mikey says quietly, trying to ignore the little voices in his head that sound a lot like the twins talking about crushes and the size thereof. "I know."

"WHAT?" Tolya asks, stopping mid-sentence.

"Huh?" Mikey asks, blinking at him from his side of the table. He'd actually been interested in the play Tolya had been describing; if they can make it work once he gets back on the ice, he can think of a couple of variations that could really take advantage of his speed and Tolya's strength.

Tolya shakes his head. "You're staring at me. Have I got something on my face?"

"Nah." Mikey shrugs. "Just listening. And, you know. It's good to have you back."

A smile spreads slowly across Tolya's face, tiny and uncertain. "I missed you, too," he says, his tone somewhere between sincerity and chirping.

The waitress arrives with their food before things can get any more serious. Mikey can't decide if he's happy about that or not.

Honestly, he blames the twins for this level of confusion. Before they showed up and started talking about crushes and feelings and shit, everything was fine. Well, maybe not fine, but good. He was getting better, he had Tolya there to take care of him, they were having awesome sex. Most of the time he could forget about the trade rumors.

"Dude, really?" he says when Tolya lifts his phone to take a picture of his plate.

"It looks good!" Tolya says.

Mikey rolls his eyes. "Yeah, it does, but seriously, your Insta is half gym selfies for your thirst followers and half pictures of plates of food. Change it up a little once in awhile."

"Oh, I guess you're a social media expert now?" Tolya chirps back, grinning. "Just because Buzzfeed did a whole listicle about your stupid dog rating pictures?"

"Watch and learn," Mikey says, pulling out his own phone.

He takes a minute to nudge their plates closer together, moving the candle centerpiece to the very edge of the frame.

"Am I done learning yet?" Tolya asks, crossing his arms.

"Art can't be rushed, Tolya." Mikey checks the layout on his phone screen, sticks his casted hand doing a clumsy thumbs-up into the foreground, and snaps the picture.

Tolya doesn't bother waiting for him to say anything, just waits as Mikey painstakingly taps out the caption— He's back! #bffdinner #goals #missedyoubro #carbloading

—and posts the photo. A few seconds later, Tolya's phone buzzes on the tabletop. Picking it up, he swipes one-handed to unlock it, twirling fettucine onto his fork with the other. "Really?" he says.

Mikey shrugs, loading gnocchi onto his fork and trying not to count the days until he can eat two-handed again. "I stand by it."

Tolya glances around, like there are Deadspin writers or paparazzi hiding in the fake bushes, and says quietly, "You know, given the amount of sex we've had, I think you could leave off the 'bro.' It just seems weird."

Before Mikey can come up with a good response for that, his phone starts going off, one notification right after another. "Oh, shit. I forgot to turn off comment notifica-tions," he groans, setting his fork down and picking up the phone again.

When he unlocks the screen, though, the notifications aren't from Instagram. Or at least, not all of them. Mostly he has a string of snap notifications from the twins.

"Everything okay?" Tolya asks.

"Yeah, it's all good," Mikey says. "The twins are sending me snaps. I'm kind of scared to open them, to be honest. Plausible deniability and all that."

Tolya laughs. "Okay, but consider this; if we need to go bail them out, we should probably know now and not after we get home."

"Point." Mikey takes a deep breath and opens Snapchat, subtly tilting his screen away from Tolya, just in case.

He must have missed the first snap; the time stamp is from a little over an hour ago. It's just the two of them in a dimly lit room with another girl who must either be Daria or some random person they grabbed off the street to give credence to their story. The caption just says "three musketeers reunited!!!!!!"

Holding his breath, he opens the next one. It's just a screenshot of his Insta post with the words "GIANT CRUSH" over it in the most obnoxious font they could find, plus hearts in every color. He closes that one as quickly as he can, only to be inundated with a series of skeptical-looking selfies from both Andrea and Diana, with increasingly ridiculous suggestions about how best to declare his love to Tolya.

The final snap is a gif of Sebastian from The Little Mermaid, captioned "KISS THE BOY!!!!"

"So how much bail money do we need?" Tolya asks at the exact moment that one disappears from the screen.

Mikey shakes himself out of his reverie, closing the app and locking his phone. "Nah, they're good. They met up with their friend and made it to the concert."

Tolya looks at him for a long moment, like he can tell there's something else going on, but clearly decides not to press the matter. "Cool."

"Yeah," Mikey echoes, turning his attention back to his food and trying not to think about romance or Disney movies or kissing. "Cool."

After first regular season game

Mikey is drunk.

Not like, where he's gonna fall down or puke or black out; college was very educational in this respect. He's got a really good idea of his limits and what it takes to find and achieve the perfect level of inebriation.

Right now he's riding that edge like a pro. Everything is warm and good and happy, the music is good, the people are attractive, and he's surrounded by his team.

"Dance with me!" he yells in Tolly's ear, leaning in close to be heard over the driving bass beat the DJ is laying down.

"Really?" Tolly asks, eyebrows raised.

Mikey grabs his hand by way of answer, pulling him out of the booth.

Yeah, sure, the dance floor is full of people, and probably some of them would dance with him if he asked, but he's still riding high on their game at least as much as on the drinks. A goal off Tolly's assist, an assist on Tolly's goal—they may only have played about ten minutes, but those ten minutes were fucking amazing. He still feels that connection between them, still wants to feel it.

Tolly goes willingly enough, lets his hands fall onto Mikey's waist when the reach the floor and Mikey turns to face him. He's about as hopeless at dancing as most white guys, but that's okay. Mikey has enough rhythm for both of them, and this isn't the kind of song for anything fancy. This is music for down and dirty grinding.

It takes Tolly a few minutes to catch on, but he doesn't

pull away, follows Mikey's lead and lets him press their bodies together, move them to the beat.

Mikey can see other guys from the team scattered around the floor if he lets his eyes wander. Mostly they're dancing with other people, but a few of them have paired up like he and Tolly have, enough that he doesn't feel awkward about it. But he doesn't spend much time looking, his attention increasingly caught by Tolya.

He knew, of course, that they're basically the same height. But he didn't know that meant Tolly's shoulders were the perfect height to loop his arms over. Or the way their bodies would line up perfectly for grinding, delicious friction that probably feels better than it should with so many layers of clothes between them. Or how tempting it would be to have Tolly's mouth only centimeters from his.

It's entirely possible that he might have been drunk enough to do it, to give into temptation and close the distance between them. But before he can quite work up the nerve, Nova and Sunshine appear next to them, pulling them back to the booth for another round of shots.

In the morning, Mikey will tell himself that it's for the best, that it's not a good idea to mess with their friendship or their on-ice chemistry.

In the morning he'll be smarter.

But right now, he wants.

15

TOLYA

"**W**e're fucking going out tonight!" Guns crows, pulling Tolya into a headlock as they clear the locker room door. "I'm not taking no for an answer, Petrov!"

"Okay, okay," Tolya says with a laugh.

Guns nods, squeezing one last time before letting go. "I already texted Mikey and told him to get his ass down here from the press box. He needs to come with us and celebrate that gorgeous fucking goal."

His face heating, Tolya shrugs, escaping to his stall to start stripping out of his gear. "It was a lucky shot," he mumbles.

"Yeah, it was," Suzie agrees. "But you took it. Even with that bullshit penalty on Sunshine in the third, we kicked Jackalopes ass!"

The roar of agreement that rises from around the room is nearly deafening. Tolya wonders if he's the only one who noticed that Sunshine didn't join in; if their stalls weren't right next to each other, he's not sure he would have either.

"Hey," he murmurs under the general hubbub, once he's sure no one else is paying attention. "You okay?"

"Huh?" Sunshine says. It takes a beat longer than it should have but eventually his eyes come back into focus. "Oh, yeah. All good."

He should probably leave it there, honestly, but Sunshine had still looked shaken when he got out of the penalty box. Even for someone known for his clean play, a two-minute penalty shouldn't rock your world like that. Especially since Suzie is right; it was absolutely bullshit. "You sure? You looked like you'd seen a ghost when you came out of the box."

Sunshine laughs, short and humorless. "I guess that's one way to put it." His expression softens when he meets Tolya's eyes. "I'm okay. Just—don't worry about it, okay?"

"Whatever you say," Tolya says, trying not to make his voice obviously skeptical.

"Please," Sunshine says, his voice almost pleading, and that—that's not right. But he looks like he might break under too much pressure right now, so Tolya just nods, doesn't push.

He's halfway out of his gear when Sarah from PR shows up, completely ignoring the various stages of nudity around her except to raise an eyebrow when Rover snaps a towel too close to her pristine slacks—he mutters an apology and slinks back to his tall. She's leading reporters, of course, and Tolya makes himself put on his best blandly pleasant expression.

That earns him an approving shoulder pat from Sarah before she abandons him to the sharks. Tolya does his best to keep his answers as basic and inoffensive as possible, takes advantage of sipping on his Gatorade when he needs a second to think about a response.

Thankfully, since they won, and he scored, the questions are mostly pretty easy to answer, the kind of thing he could come up with in his sleep. Yes, he's pleased with the goal, yes, his point totals are good. Yes, the defense needs to tighten up a little but they're working hard on that, every practice. Yes, Tiger's shutout was amazing and they're lucky to have him. He even manages to sidestep a question about Sunshine's penalty without outright calling the refs fucking blind.

Of course, as soon as he slips into complacency, he gets fucking blindsided.

"What do you think about the Michaelson trade rumors?" the reporter asks, pushing a recorder a little closer to his face. "You and Carson seem to have been clicking better in recent games; do you think that will affect management's decision?"

Tolya thanks whatever gods are listening that he already had the Gatorade halfway to his mouth, although he's a little worried about swallowing anything around the giant lump in his throat. The drink seems to be over in a flash, and then he still has to answer. Shit.

"Come on," he says, doing his best not to grit his teeth, to make his expression look more like a smile and less like an aggressive baring of teeth. "I'm not in the front office, I don't have the C, or even an A. I'm just a rookie. You think they're telling me what they're thinking? Your guess is as good as mine; probably better."

Unfortunately, the reporter seems determined to push it. "But surely you have an opinion? Especially since Michaelson was your defensive partner."

"My opinion," Tolya says slowly, doing his best to make eye contact with someone, anyone, who can rescue him before he decks this asshole, and not to react to him already talking about Misha in the past tense. "My opinion is that Mi-Mikey is one of my best friends, and one of the best d-partners I've had. I'm lucky I don't have to be the person to make that call, like I said."

"But do you think—"

"That's all for tonight, folks," Sarah says briskly, herding the reporters out of the locker room through some force-field magic they must teach PR people in college. "Thanks for coming, you can contact me for any follow-up questions or interviews…" Her voice trails off as the locker room door swings closed behind her.

Tolya sits there. He's aware of the sound and move-ment around him, of the wet, sodden weight of his gear on his body, almost unbearably hot. But he can't move, can barely breathe, all but crushed under the weight of reality.

"Hey," someone says, but he doesn't look, not until a shoulder bumps into his, hard.

"Now you look like you've seen a ghost," Sunshine says. "You okay?"

Tolya shrugs. Is he okay? Who knows?

"Come on," Sunshine says gently. "Get showered, get dressed. You don't wanna keep Mikey waiting, do you?"

And that—yeah. Tolya forces his hands to move, to finish stripping off the last of his gear. A part of him is embarrassed that Sunshine can read him so easily, that he's so obvious. But mostly he's simply, almost pathetically grateful.

He stands under the hot water for as long as he can stand, letting the stink and sweat of the game swirl down the drain with the bubbles of lather, and does his best not to think about the future.

"You had a great game!" Misha yells in his ear. He has to lean in to do it, so close his lips brush the shell of Tolya's ear, just to be heard over the pounding bass line the DJ is using. "That goal was fucking filthy!"

Tolya shrugs, doing his best to project normalcy. Calm. Nothing to see here. "I got lucky."

Misha shakes his head, stays right where his is, warm

and solid and present against Tolya's side. "Nope. Anyway, you always say luck is mostly preparation."

"Yeah, okay," Tolya says, taking another drink of his beer.

"Drink up!" Guns yells, somehow managing to set down four shot glasses on the table without spilling anything. "You've got more to get through, Tolly!"

Tolya sighs. "We have practice in the morning, Guns. I don't wanna puke on the ice."

"Fine," Guns says cheerfully, waving Orange and Rover toward the table to take a shot glass each and giving Misha a sympathetic look. "One shot, and then we'll keep the rest of these drinks to ourself."

"One shot," Tolya agrees, grabbing the glass and taking a cautious sniff. "Shit, man. Vodka? Who do you think I am, Nova?"

Guns rolls his eyes. "The tequila here is shit. Just drink up, whiny. Bottoms up!"

"Bottoms up," Tolya echoes, Rover and Orange chiming in a second behind, and throws back the shot as fast as he can.

He's never liked the taste of straight vodka, much to his dad's horror (and insistence that *good* vodka, *Russian* vodka, has no taste). It burns going down his throat, but that's not necessarily a bad thing. The physical discomfort, the way it blends with the buzz from his one and a half beers so far, is at least a distraction from—

Dragging his attention away from that thought, he thunks the shot glass back down on the table. "We good?"

he asks Guns, letting himself lean into Misha just a little bit.

Of course, this is Guns, so he gets pulled into some kind of weird bro-hug-turned-secret-handshake combo where he has no idea what he's doing, but that never seems to matter. "We're good!" Guns says, turning toward the dance floor. "I'm going to dance!"

Looking out over the relatively sparse crowd—on a weeknight it's nothing like as packed as it would be on a Friday or Saturday night—Tolya can see that most of the team is already out there. Some of them have significant others with them, the ones who haven't already gone home, and most of the single guys are either dancing in pairs and small clusters or have found someone who's caught their eye.

Aside from Tolya and Misha, the only two people left in the VIP balcony are Sunshine, staring morosely into half a beer, and Lindy, who's draining the last of his drink and heading for the stairs down to the dance floor.

"Hey," Tolya says, leaning in so Misha can hear him. "Do you know what's up with Sunshine?"

"Sunshine?" Misha looks over to where Sunshine is still attempting to read his future in beer foam or whatever. "No, he seemed fine before the game. What's up?"

Tolya shakes his head. "I don't know. He's been weird ever since that penalty, but he didn't want me to push it, and then the reporters showed up, asking—"

He clamps his mouth shut, but it's too late. Misha's not stupid, and he's not exhausted from playing a game, or halfway to buzzed. A muscle jumps in his jaw as he puts two and two together. "Asking about me getting traded, huh?"

"Yeah," Tolya admits, reaching for his beer because all he wants is to reach for Misha instead, to hold him and be held in return. But this is a public club; literally anyone with a camera phone could take their picture and sell it to the press. The only thing he wants less than to be asked about his friend being traded is to be asked about his—his what? What are they even to each other?

Shit.

"Anyway," he says, when he can talk without feeling like he's about to choke on his words. "Something's up with Sunshine. You should talk to him."

"I will," Misha agrees. "But this isn't exactly a great place for a heart-to-heart. And I kinda want to go home now. I'm gonna get a Lyft."

Tolya considers draining the last of his beer, but thinks better of it. "I'll come with you," he says.

For a second he wonders if it came out too eager, too obvious with his stupid feelings written on his sleeve. If Misha even wants him there. But then Misha smiles at him and he doesn't even care.

"Okay," Misha says simply, offering him a hand as he slides out of the booth.

It's dark, but that's not the only reason Tolya holds onto his hand all the way home.

INSTEAD OF HEADING for the elevators when they enter the lobby, Misha leads him to the back exit, out into the small green space for apartment residents, now brown and dead, frost sparkling on the grass. There's no one out here, of course, it's dark and cold, even if this winter has been pretty mild so far, even if Christmas is just around the corner. But Tolya doesn't resist when Misha heads toward the small children's playground, keeping their hands joined as he sits down on one of the swings.

Tolya takes the other one. They sit in silence for a while, still holding hands as the swings move gently in the dark. The city moves around them, traffic sounds and people laughing, but this moment is still, the eye of the storm.

"They're gonna trade me," Misha says finally, his words stark in the previously silent space.

"They won't," Tolya says, but it sounds flat and false even to him. Too little, too late.

Misha shakes his head. "I've got another two weeks before the cast comes off, and then I have to do physio and rehab. I'm not going to be ready to play for a month, minimum. Could be longer. And there's no telling how I'll be playing then. Trading me is the smart thing. If they can find anyone who'll even take me."

"Misha," Tolya says helplessly. He's too drunk for this, but maybe there's no way he could be sober enough for this. For Misha's voice, bitterness and pain and hopeless fear suffusing every word. "They—"

"You know what?" Misha interrupts. "I don't think I

want to talk about this after all. I want to go upstairs and I want to fuck you into the mattress."

Tolya chokes on air, doing his best to follow the quick turn this conversation has taken. But in the end, with Misha watching him, eyes bright with emotion and the unspoken question hanging in the air between them—

—in the end, there's only one answer he was ever going to give.

After their first roadie

"Sunshine! Buy-in's fifty dollars," Bucky says when Cisco sits down across from him.

"Do I get to know what we're betting on?" he asks, poking at his chicken breast and doing his best not to bemoan his aging metabolism.

Bucky grins, wide and innocent. "When the rookies are gonna stop eye-fucking and actually fuck. Rover says by the start of December."

"What's the pool up to?" Cisco asks, giving in and taking a bite of chicken. The rice is decently seasoned, at least, but he really has to start bringing lunch from home so he doesn't have to eat this bland-ass white people food. "And don't you assholes have anything better to do?"

"Seven hundred," Bucky says. "And no, obviously. In or out, Sunshine."

He sighs, digging out his phone and opening Venmo. "Fine. What do you have left?"

Bucky shoves a paper calendar and a pen in his direction, stuffing broccoli into his face with his other hand.

After flipping through the pages for a moment and shaking his head over some of the notations—there's no way Mikey and Tolly are going to make it to April, no matter what Guns thinks—Cisco pencils his initials in on December thirteenth and pushes the calendar back across the table to Bucky.

"Pleasure doing business with you," Bucky says, making the calendar disappear somehow as Mikey and Tolly sit down at the next table over.

Watching the way they laugh together, Cisco starts to think maybe they won't even make it until December.

Mikey manages, barely, to keep his hands to himself on the elevator ride. It's hard as hell, with Tolya standing *right there*. His shoulder presses firmly into Mikey's firm even through the bulk of their winter coats, but it's not enough to sate the sharp-edged need rising up like an unstoppable wave.

He's a little afraid he might drown in it. He's more afraid of how attractive that prospect is.

Their apartment door is still sliding closed behind them when his control finally snaps. He pushes Tolya up against the wall with his good hand, keeping him there with the pressure of his body.

The kiss is different from any they've had before, all hunger and teeth and need. Tolya meets him with an equal intensity, like maybe he's feeling some of the same desperation that's clawing at Mikey. They kiss until Mikey feels light-headed from the need to breathe, until he can't take the frustration of his hands slipping off the slick surface of Tolya's coat another second.

"Off," he demands, pulling back enough to fumble at the zipper, yanking it down with vicious force. Their arms tangle for a second when Tolya does the same for him, but then the coats are abandoned somewhere on the floor and he can plaster himself against Tolya again, can slide his hands under the jacket of his game day suit, can feel the warmth of skin bleeding through the thin fabric of his shirt.

Mikey dives back in for another kiss, hotter and wetter and somehow even more desperate, fisting his hand in Tolya's shirt and yanking it free of his waistband, reaching underneath to find skin. He can feel Tolya's cock against his hip, hard and hot even through the fabric of their slacks, Tolya's hands framing his face, the shiver that runs through Tolya's body when he bites down on his lip.

Tearing his mouth away, Mikey drags his mouth down to the hinge of Tolya's jaw, pausing to bite and suck at the sensitive spot under his ear until the skin is hot under his tongue, until Tolya's hands are just digging into his back, desperately holding on.

When he lifts his head, the mark blooming there has a dark satisfaction curling in his stomach. But it's not enough. "Bed," he demands, circling his good hand around Tolya's wrist and towing him down the hallway toward the bedrooms.

They end up in Mikey's because it's closer, but that's good, too, that he'll have the memory of this in his bed. Tolya goes willingly when Mikey pushes him toward the bed, only pausing to take Mikey's hand and lift it to his mouth, pressing a kiss to the palm. "Whatever you need," he murmurs, his eyes wide and dark. "Anything, Misha."

Mikey clamps down on the surge of emotion. "I need us to be naked," he says hoarsely, taking his hand back to start fumbling with his shirt buttons.

Tolya bats his hands away and starts undoing them himself, faster with his two good hands than Mikey would be with one. His movements are just as urgent as Mikey's, but more focused, more efficient. He gets Mikey's shirt open, his cuffs unbuttoned, before reaching for his own, leaving Mikey to shrug out of his shirt and undo his slacks.

By the time Mikey's down to his boxers, clumsily shoving them down, Tolya's completely naked. He steps in to cover Mikey's hands with his own, and together they push the underwear down. Mikey steps out of them, abandoning them to lie puddled on the floor, Tolya's hands on his waist to steady him, and keeps walking, guiding Tolya back toward the bed.

"What do you want, Misha?" Tolya asks, his voice hoarse, as his legs hit the mattress.

"I told you what I want," Mikey says, following him onto the bed. The mark he left on Tolya's neck is darker now; he's going to get chirped for that at practice in the morning, but Mikey just wants more. Wants Tolya's paler skin covered in hickies and bite marks and beard burn, the indelible evidence that Mikey was here, that they were both here. Together.

Something of this must show on his face, something of all the things he can't say, that he can't look at head-on. Tolya reaches for him, pulling him down until he's stretched out on top of Tolya, settled between his thighs, skin to skin, heartbeat to heartbeat, his face buried in the side of Tolya's neck.

"You want to fuck me?" Tolya murmurs, lifting a leg to wrap it around Mikey's waist. "I'm here. You can. Whatever you want, baby."

Mikey shudders at the words, at the feeling. "I don't— I want—I don't want to hurt you."

Tolya chuckles, low and throaty. "Unless you have some kind of secret blood fetish I don't know about, you're not gonna hurt me worse than I get in practice or a game, Misha. Come on. I can take it. I want to, for you."

Shuddering again, Mikey drags his mouth down the side of Tolya's neck, pleased when that gets him an answering shiver. He bites down on the swell of Tolya's traps, gently at first, then harder when Tolya moans an affirmative, arching up under him.

After that, he maybe loses his mind a little, slipping into a fugue state where the only thing that matters is the next spot to leave his mark on Tolya, the next sound he can pull from Tolya's mouth, the next reaction to read in Tolya's body. His nipples are sensitive, Mikey discovers, enough so that just dragging his beard over them is enough to have Tolya squirming and breathless under him. Licking and sucking gets him moans and begging, the frantic movement of Tolya's hips as he searches for friction on his cock.

Mikey almost, almost wants to linger there, to see how far he can push it, if he can make Tolya come just from that. But there's so much of Tolya left to explore, so he moves on. Down, across abs so ticklish that Tolya begs for the first time, breathless with what can only be described as giggles. Down, following the deep v groove leading, always, to his cock, flushed red and standing hard.

That's not his objective, though Mikey can't resist one lingering lick over the head, savoring the salty-bitter flavor there, before continuing onward. Tolya goes easily when Mikey pushes at his thighs, folding them back toward his chest so Mikey can leave a string of biting kisses down his hamstrings.

"Lube?" Mikey asks, unable to tear his eyes away from the marks of his mouth on Tolya's skin.

Tolya shifts under his hands, a drawer opens and closes, and Tolya hands him the lube, drops a condom packet on the bed next to him. "I can—" he starts.

"I want to—I want to try," Mikey says. He wants this, *needs* to do this, but despite the driving drumbeat of need under his skin, he's not going to call things off if he can't manage one-handed.

Tolya nods, settling back against the pillows again. "Want me to turn over?"

Mikey shakes his head, managing to open the lube without much trouble. "No, I—I want to see you."

He drizzles lube over his fingers, making a mess on the sheets, but fuck, it's not like they weren't going to be covered in jizz anyway. A little lube isn't going to make it worse. Thanking whatever gods might be listening that his arm is healed enough to move his right hand a little, he reaches down, spreading Tolya open and rubbing a tentative finger over the tight furl of his hole.

"This okay?" he asks.

When he tears his eyes away to look up at Tolya's face, renewed arousal hits like a bolt of lightning down his spine. Tolya looks wrecked already, teeth digging into his lower lip, his hair a mess, a hot flush spreading from his cheeks down his neck and across his chest. But even on his flushed skin, the marks of Mikey's attention stand out like beacons.

"Yeah," Tolya breathes, his eyes wide and dark, his hands coming down to hook behind his knees, holding himself even more open. "Yeah, Misha, please—"

"Okay," Mikey replies. He has to look away; if he looks at Tolya's face, there's no way he'll be able to focus enough to make this good for Tolya. "Okay, I've got you."

It's a strange feeling, ignoring his own arousal while working Tolya slowly open with his left hand. He'd thought it would make more of a difference, it being the left, like it did with jerking himself off. But, maybe because he's never done this with a guy before, it doesn't seem to be a problem. At least, not judging from the little punched-out noises Tolya makes with each thrust, the way his whole body goes taut when Mikey finally finds his prostate.

"Please," he finally gasps when Mikey has three fingers moving smoothly in and out. "Please, Misha—I'm gonna—I don't want to come yet. Not until—"

Mikey shudders all over at the words, at the mental picture. One day, he promises himself, he's going to do that, to make Tolya come from just his touch. But not today. "Okay," he says, indulging himself with one last thrust before pulling his fingers free.

He reaches for the condom packet and immediately realizes the problem. "Uh—"

"Here, give it," Tolya says impatiently, reaching for the packet. His hands slip a little on the traces of lube Mikey's fingers left on the foil, but he tears it open quickly, rolling it over Mikey's cock with quick, impatient hands. "Come on, come on."

"Wait," Mikey says, reaching for the lube and slicking himself up quickly before allowing Tolya to pull him in with a leg around his waist.

Pushing inside is just as incredible as he remembered , slick, tight heat around his cock. He tries to go slowly, to take it easy, but Tolya is just as desperate as he is, bucking his hips up when Mikey stops, and taking him halfway in one movement.

"Oh, fuck," Tolya groans, throwing his head back on the pillow. "Misha, come on, I thought you were gonna fuck me."

Biting the inside of his cheek to try and hold back the waves of arousal breaking over him, Mikey withdraws, then thrusts in again with a snap of his hips. "Like that?"

"Yes," Tolya moans, his eyes sliding shut with the next thrust. "Harder, Misha. Wanna feel it tomorrow—"

Mikey does his best to comply, bracing his good hand on the mattress and fucking into Tolya with all of his strength. The moans and cries and curses falling from Tolya's lips spur him on, until he's shaking with every thrust, determined not to come until Tolya does. "Come on," he pants. "Come on, Tolya, sweetheart, want you to come for me—"

He loses his words when Tolya comes, hot and tight around his cock, splattering across his abs and up onto his chest. The steady rhythm he was holding onto dissolves into frantic, desperate thrusts as he chases his own orgasm, fast and fierce when it finally rips through him.

The first thing he notices when awareness of his body returns is that he's face-planted in Tolya's chest, his nose inches from the sparse blond wisps of Tolya's chest hair. One of Tolya's hands strokes up and down his back, while the other combs rhythmically through his hair.

"I'm never moving again," Mikey announces, the words muffled against Tolya's skin.

"Okay," Tolya says agreeably, his hands never pausing in their steady movements. "But you're the one who has to call and explain that I can't come to practice because we're stuck together with dried jizz."

Mikey snorts. "You think I won't?"

"No, I know you will," Tolya says with a laugh. "But also this might be a little awkward when your parents show up for Christmas."

"Shit." Mikey jolts upright with barely a wince when yes, half-dried jizz pulls at the trail of hair down his stomach, trying in vain to keep him connected to Tolya. "How the fuck did I forget about Christmas?"

Tolya shrugs lazily, only making the slightest face when Mikey's softening cock slips out of him. "You've had a lot going on. You just got distracted."

Actually, Mikey is a little distracted at this very moment. Tolya looks like porn, sprawled out on his bed, covered in jizz, looking like he's just gotten fucked within an inch of his life—which, actually, he kind of has. The marks Mikey left are even darker than the last time he looked, and he can't resist reaching out with his good hand, brushing his fingertips over the purpling bruise under Tolya's ear.

"How bad is it?" Tolya asks, not looking all that concerned.

"Um." Mikey's aware that he should probably feel guilty, and he does. Kind of. But the guilt is mostly eclipsed by a deep satisfaction. "I mean, what's bad, really?"

Tolya rolls his eyes, sitting up in one fluid movement. "I look like I got attacked by a vampire wannabe, don't I?"

"Little bit." Mikey touches the bite mark on his collarbone. "I maybe kind of got a little carried away. Sorry?"

"No you aren't," Tolya says, heading for the bathroom, and the big mirror there. "Jesus fuck, Misha!"

Mikey considers running, but there's no point; Tolya would catch him easily. Reluctantly, he walks toward the bathroom, stepping inside just as Tolya presses on one of the marks, hissing between his teeth.

"None of my shirts are going to cover this one," he says when he spots Mikey, gesturing to the one on his neck. "You owe me so big."

"Whatever you say," Mikey agrees, walking up behind him and wrapping his good arm around his waist.

Tolya shakes his head, but he's smiling. "Let me get the plastic bag so we can shower. And Misha?"

"Yeah?"

"You're going to have a matching one for Christmas."

Mikey shivers a little at the thought, electricity jolting down his spine. "That's not really a threat," he calls as Tolya leaves the bathroom.

The words float back to him. "I know."

As soon as Mikey opens the door, still rubbing at his eyes, the twins nearly knock him off his feet. "It's Christmas!" they chorus, and for a second he's nine again, jostled awake at an ungodly hour by two four-year-olds jumping on his bed like they're practicing for the Olympics.

"It's Christmas!" he replies, managing to keep his feet somehow and smiling over their heads at his parents, despite the fact that it's barely six in the morning. "Come in!"

The next few minutes are a flurry of hugs and trying not to step on each other's feet as they flood into the apartment. It's not that there are a lot of people, it's just that all four of his family members are carrying a truly ridiculous number of shopping bags and other containers. Mikey tries to take some, but even Andrea won't relinquish hers.

"You just sit down," his mom says, dropping a kiss on his cheek as she bustles by, setting a crock-pot on the counter and plugging it in. "Don't worry, next year we'll put you to work, assuming you have two working hands."

"You know what they say about assumptions, Mom," Diana says with a smirk.

His mom levels an intimidating kitchen knife she found from somewhere in Diana's direction. "I do, young lady. You might consider if that's something you want to say to your mother."

Diana holds up her hands in surrender, joining Andrea at the tree as they start unloading a small mountain of presents.

"You didn't have to cook, Mrs. Michaelson," Tolya interjects, thankfully changing the subject. "We could've gotten a meal delivered."

"First of all, how many times do I have to tell you to call me Erika?" Mikey's mom says, turning to Tolya with a sunny smile. "And secondly, don't worry about it. Since you boys can't make it home for Christmas, we're bringing home to you. When did you say your parents were going to get here?"

Tolya smiles back. "They got in last night, but they should be here any minute. Is there something I can help with, since Misha is on the injured list?"

"You absolutely can," his mom says with an approving look. "I'm going to save a burner for your mother, because she said she was going to make something—pierogies?"

"Piroshki," Tolya corrects. "They're similar to pierogies, but they usually have a meat filling. In the meantime, how can I help?"

Mikey settles in on one of the barstools with his cup of coffee, watching with bemusement while his mom marshals his dad and Tolya like a general preparing for battle. Within a few minutes Tolya is cutting a pork roast into careful cubes and his dad is chopping a small mountain of onions and peppers. That done, his mom starts the corn husks soaking, then produces a large mixing bowl from somewhere and starts mixing the masa with lard and all the other good things that go into tamales.

Even with only half a cup of coffee in him, Mikey can tell exactly when his parents notice the fading hickey on Tolya's neck. He waits, holding his breath, as they exchange a look—

And nothing happens.

Just as Mikey is about to give in and say something stupid, someone knocks on the door. "I'll get it," he says, sliding to his feet and padding over to the door in his sock feet, not sure if he's feeling relief or regret. If he wants to keep things secret a little longer, or if he's ready to have it out in the open.

"Happy Christmas!" Vladislav booms as soon as the door cracks open.

"I'm sorry," his wife, Ana says as they come through the door Mikey holds open for them. "I told him it was a ridiculous hour."

From the kitchen, Mikey's mom says, "Good food takes time! Come in, come in!"

"Exactly!" Vladislav says, pulling Mikey into a bear hug and kissing him once on each cheek before letting go. "This is what I say!"

Mikey catches Tolya's eye and sees his own combination of embarrassment and happiness reflected there. It's just for a second, before Tolya is engulfed in hugs from his parents—like they hadn't seen each other last night—and there are two more bodies in the kitchen.

"Good thing we didn't get the other place," Mikey says when Tolya joins him at the bar. Trying to imagine all four of their parents fitting into the tiny kitchenette of the other condo they'd looked at before is a mind-boggling exercise.

"Yeah," Tolya agrees, smiling back at him.

The apartment is already starting to fill with smells that make his mouth water. His family is here. Tolya is here.

Right now, everything is good.

"Presents?" Andrea asks, looking way too alert for someone who has just finished eating basically her body weight in tamales and other food.

"Patience, grasshopper," their dad says, groaning a little when he tries to move. "None of us are as young as we used to be."

The twins roll their eyes in unison before turning pleading looks on Mikey and Tolya. "We've been waiting all day. You're not *that* old yet. Come *on*," Diana says, making her best Puss-in-Boots eyes at them.

Tolya grins at Mikey. "I don't know, I'm feeling kind of full. How about you?"

"Super full," Mikey agrees, returning the grin. "Might be like, an hour before I can move. I was injured, you know."

"Oh my *God,*" Andrea says, flouncing off to the couch, Diana on her heels.

Eventually, after the leftovers are put away to the satisfaction of both moms, who seem to have come to a slightly terrifying understanding, everyone gathers in the living area around the slightly-lopsided Christmas tree.

The twins distribute the boxes and envelopes and packages with brisk, intimidating efficiency, clearly working from a predetermined plan of attack. Once all the gifts have been sorted, they dive into their own pile, ripping and tearing with violent abandon, looking about ten years younger than their actual age.

"Remember when Christmas was that exciting?" Tolya asks, nudging Mikey with a gentle elbow.

Mikey raises his eyebrows. "Are you saying you're not excited to open my thoughtfully selected present? I'm hurt, *Anatoly*."

"I don't see you rushing to open *my* perfect gift, *Kevin*," Tolya retorts.

"Quit flirting and open them already!" Andrea snaps, holding up the sweater she's just pulled from a box in her lap. "Thanks, Mamí, it's perfect."

Their mom sighs. "Yes, dear. Stop heckling your brother and Tolya and open the rest of your presents."

Distracted by the argument, Mikey almost doesn't notice Tolya starting to unwrap his present until he catches movement in the corner of his eye. And of course Tolya is one of those people who unwraps like an old grandma, carefully undoing the tape and folding the wrapping paper back to reveal the innocent-looking white box in the center.

"I had to pay for the gift-wrapping, obviously," Mikey says. "Which is good, because it wouldn't have looked that nice even if I had both hands working. Just ask Mom, or the twins. It's a mess. I never got the hang of it—"

He can feel more babble rising up in his throat like vomit, but the look on Tolya's face as he lifts the leather jacket stops it. The twins look over at the same moment, eyebrows raised.

"You got him a jacket, Kevin? Wow," Andrea says, her voice supremely unimpressed.

"It's a replica of Captain America's jacket from the Avengers movie," Tolya tells her, never looking up from where he's running his hands over the butter-soft leather. "Where did you find this?"

Mikey shrugs, trying to ignore the heat rising up in his cheeks, and the looks from the twins and both sets of parents. "There's a company that makes them, but they're custom-sized; I had to steal one of your suit jackets to get the measurements."

All of the effort and the sneaking is worth it, in this moment, watching Tolya slide his arms into the jacket and smile like he hasn't since the day Mikey woke up in the hospital. "Does it fit okay?" Mikey asks, just for something to say, even though he can clearly see that it does.

"It's perfect," Tolya says.

When he leans in, Mikey meets him halfway, and despite the catcalling from his sisters, he has to agree.

It's perfect.

"Open yours," Tolya says when he pulls back, smiling softly.

Mikey complies, at least as much to avoid looking at the embarrassing facial expression his mom is sure to be making as because he's excited to see what Tolya got him. He rips into the surprisingly solid package gleefully, still trying to figure out what it is—there was remarkably little rattling when he shook it.

As it turns out when he gets through the wrapping paper, it's two packages wrapped together. "Really?" he says, looking up at Tolya. "I'm still in a cast here, you know."

"I mean, if you don't want both of them—"

Mikey wraps his arms protectively around the packages. "Back off!"

Ignoring the laughter around them—seriously, do their family members not have anything to do other than watch them?—Mikey sets aside the smaller package and starts tearing the paper on the larger one. It's hard with his left hand, but he's still able to get it open pretty quickly, revealing a stack of books with familiar covers.

"We're almost done with *Night Watch*," Tolya says. "I thought I'd let you pick which one you want to start next."

Mikey has to blink a little rapidly at that before he can answer. Realistically, he knows Tolya doesn't have any control over whether or not he gets traded. But sitting here, surrounded by their respective families, holding a stack of at least five books, it feels different. It feels like a promise. "That—that sounds good."

"You can open the other one later, if you want," Tolya murmurs, quietly enough that hopefully no one else will catch it. His cheeks are pink, like maybe it's something embarrassing?

Before Mikey can decide, Diana swoops the package up and starts shaking it like the annoying child she somehow still is. "What's this one?"

"Give me that!" He snatches it back from her after several tries.

"Well?" She says, watching expectantly. "Open it!"

He tears at the paper more slowly this time, holding his breath as a jeweler's box comes into view. "What?"

"It's probably dumb," Tolya mutters.

Now nearly bursting with curiosity, Mikey finishes peeling away the paper and opens the box. He catches his breath at the sight of the silver snowflakes nestled on dark blue satin.

"They're cufflinks," Tolya says, one hand rubbing over the back of his neck. "Remember, last time we went to the tailor he said you should get some, and I saw those at the store, and thought you'd like them."

"Wow," Mikey says, reaching out to touch one snowflake gently. "They're amazing."

Andrea makes gagging sounds, helpfully reminding him that they have an audience. "Does this mean we have to start calling you Elsa now? I still have the wig if you need it."

"Wig?" Tolya asks, looking entirely too curious.

Maybe the timing of Mikey pulling him in for a kiss is a little suspect, but he doesn't care. And he doesn't think Tolya does, either.

First day of apartment hunting

Mikey snaps a picture of the condo's living area and texts it to his mom. It only takes about a minute before his phone starts ringing.

"You can't be serious," his mom says without preamble.

"Morning, mamí," he says. "Como esta?"

Her huff is audible even through the phone. "Mijo, *that kitchen is microscopic. Can even one person fit in there?"*

"Sure they can," he says. "And we really only need one person at a time. You know I don't cook much."

"But what about visits? Holidays?"

He rolls his eyes at Tolly. "Mamí, *we're two single guys. You really think we're going to be hosting holidays?"*

"You never know," she says. "You should find another place. Maybe you should wait until a weekend when I can come up and help you look—"

"The realtor has some questions for us," he interrupts. "I have to go. Te amo."

He's probably going to get in trouble later for how quickly he hangs up, but as much as he loves his mom, the last thing he needs is her picking his apartment for him.

"So," the realtor says, finishing her own phone call and rejoining them in the living area. "What do we think?"

"The kitchen is kinda small," Tolly says, shooting Mikey an amused glance.

"Yeah," Mikey agrees. "And I'd like to have my own bathroom."

She smiles at them, every inch the professional. "Well, then, I think I know just the place."

"You ready for this?" Tolya asks as they step out the apartment door and head for the elevator.

"So fucking ready," Misha replies, grinning wider than Tolya has seen in weeks, maybe months. "This is gonna kick ass! I just wish I was playing."

Tolya bumps their shoulders together. "Soon enough. Focus on the positive. You're coming with us this time instead of staying home."

"Yeah," Misha says, following Tolya onto the elevator as the doors open. "You're right. This is good."

And it is. It's good to have Misha with him on the drive to the airport, cracking jokes and making sure his phone downloads everything he needs for the flight.

"Mikey!" Angel yells, getting up from his seat to pull

Misha in for a hug. "Good to see you, man! How're you feeling?"

Tolya hovers while Misha makes small talk, accepting the hugs and back slaps and affection as the rest of the team arrives. Even Sunshine looks happy to see him, even if he's still acting weird otherwise. Maybe Mikey can get him to spill what's bothering him, because nobody else has had much luck.

Conversation flows easily, and probably Tolya is imagining that it seems better than it did when Misha was gone. The ones who weren't at their apartment for the fateful pizza party must have been warned, because no one even comes close to mentioning the trade rumors, even if Tolya can practically feel it hanging over their heads, dangling and waiting to fall.

But even with that looming, it's good. Misha's presence beside him as they file onto the plane and settle into their seats eases an ache Tolya hadn't realized he was feeling. It's good, plugging their headphones into the splitter Tolya hasn't needed for the last three roadies, finally getting back to their Leverage rewatch. Good to have Misha beside him on the shuttle to the arena, even if he can't really practice.

"Soon," Tolya promises, barely resisting the urge to lean in and kiss him as they part ways, as Tolya heads off with the rest of the team to dress for practice.

Every time he looks over at the boards and sees Misha there, watching, he smiles. Just having him there is amazing, and Tolya does his best not to think about the chance that he could be gone again any time.

He thinks he's doing a pretty good job, until they head back to the hotel to eat and rest before the game, Misha settled into the seat next to him on the shuttle, exactly where he should be. Maybe Tolya glares a little when Guns and Peso start talking about a trade between the Basilisks and the Reapers, but no one seems to notice.

The rest of the trip passes without incident and Tolya's already deep into his pre-game headspace when they get up to their room, so it takes him a minute to react when Misha shoves him down to sit on the foot of one bed.

"You need to chill," Misha says—growls, really.

Tolya blinks up at him. "What?"

"I'm worried, too," Misha admits, his voice softening. "But we can't change whatever shit happens between now and the trade deadline. And playing like shit because your worried isn't going to do you any favors."

"I—" Tolya stops to think about it. "You're right. I just—"

Misha nods, stepping in closer. "Yeah, I know. Want a blowjob to take your mind off it?"

That hadn't been what Tolya was angling for at all, but his cock definitely doesn't mind the idea, perking up under his sweats. "You know if we win tonight, this has to be part of the routine from now on."

Misha rolls his eyes, already sinking to his knees and tugging at the waistband of Tolya's pants. "I think I'll take that chance."

Tolya lifts his hips and helps Misha push his sweats

down. "You say that now, but when I'm pulling you into a closet at the arena—"

"Oh my God, shut up and let me blow you," Misha says, but he's laughing as he wraps his hand around the base of Tolya's cock and leans down to close his mouth over the head.

As usual, the wet heat of Misha's mouth negates at least half of Tolya's higher brain functions, but he can't bring himself to care. It's not like he was using them for anything important.

Anyway, nothing is more important than this, the silky texture of Misha's hair under his hands, the wet noises as Misha takes him deeper and deeper, the way Misha's lips stretch wide around his cock. Right now, this one endless moment is all that matters.

Within a ridiculously short amount of time, Tolya notices the warning signs. "Gonna come," he warns. Not that he thinks Misha is going to pull off, but it's polite.

Sure enough, Misha just takes him deeper, bobs his head faster, sucks harder, like he's demanding Tolya's orgasm. He gets it, too. Tolya comes with a groan, his fingers clenching in Misha's hair, shuddering as Misha licks and sucks him through it.

"Off, off," he finally says, tugging Misha up and off his cock, when he's so sensitive the gentle suction of Misha's mouth is almost painful. "C'mere, let me get you."

Misha comes willingly enough, straddling Tolya's waist and kissing him long and deep. Tolya can taste the bitter-salty remnants of his own orgasm on Misha's tongue, which should probably not be as hot as it was, but whatever. He's feeling too good to worry about it.

"Come on," Tolya says, breaking the kiss. "Lie down, let me."

Making little grumbling noises, Misha lets himself be nudged down onto the bed, only to arch up off it a little when Tolya settles between his legs, pulls his pants down far enough to free his cock, and sucks him down.

From the feel of Misha's cock, the taste of pre-come on the head, this isn't going to take much. Tolya pulls out all his best tricks: swirls his tongue around the shaft and uses it to toy with the edge of the foreskin, flicks over the sensitive spot just under the head.

"Fuck," Misha gasps, his hips bucking up off the bed as he thrusts into Tolya's mouth. "Fuck, Tolya, please—"

Tolya hums encouragingly, redoubling his efforts.

"Oh, fuck," Misha breathes, his good hand clenching on Tolya's shoulder. "I'm gonna—"

And he does, flooding Tolya's mouth as he comes. Tolya stays with him, swallowing until there's nothing left to swallow, then finally letting Misha's cock slip free and moving up to stretch out next to him on the bed.

Misha rolls toward him, nestling into his side. "Nap time?"

"Yeah," Tolya confirms. "Except we're laying on the duvet."

"Shit." Misha nuzzles his face into Tolya's shoulder. "Gimme a sec."

Tolya strokes a hand down his back, enjoying the

warmth of his body through the soft fabric of his t-shirt. It's vaguely ridiculous, both of them lying there in t-shirts and sweats shoved down around their legs, but it's not like there's anyone to see. Thanks to his post-orgasm feeling of well-being, he can't bring himself to care.

"Yeah," he says, turning his head to press a kiss to Misha's hair. "We'll move in a sec."

They very nearly fall asleep like that. In fact, Tolya's pretty sure he does doze off for a little while. But eventually the cooler air on his bare skin gets him up and moving, shifting both of them over to the other bed and under the covers.

It only takes a few seconds of that, Misha curled up warm against his side, for him to fall asleep for real

WAKING up with Misha in his arms the next morning would be pretty damn good if their conversation and the trade deadline weren't hanging over their heads like an ominous cloud over the prairie, dark and roiling. They rub off against each other in the shower, fast and desperate, hungry kisses and grabbing hands and bitten-off words, then dress and head downstairs for breakfast.

Thankfully Misha steers them to a table where Sunshine is already sitting, his resting bitch face a stark contrast to his nickname and usual smiles. He greets them with a grunt and a nod, returning his attention to the plate of eggs and potatoes in front of him. So at least they don't have to deal with a lot of questions or conversation. But that means they eat in near-total silence, enough so that Tolya catches worried looks from Stewie and Suzie. Angel, too, but his might actually be directed at Sunshine.

Their flight home is similarly quiet, with Misha speaking only when he has to. The rest of the team lets him be, giving him enough space that maybe only Tolya notices that the sadness is starting to transmute into anger.

The drive home from the airport completes the transformation. By the time they pull into their parking spot in the garage, Misha is well and truly in a mood the likes of which Tolya doesn't think he's ever seen before.

"I can get it," he snaps when Tolya reaches for the handle of his suitcase. "My left hand works just fine."

Tolya bites back a comment along the lines of, *is that why I've been jerking you off for weeks,* because that's not fucking productive and they need to not do whatever this is in public. Instead he turns toward the elevators without a word. He can practically feel the sullen anger radiating off Misha as he follows, as they ride up to their floor in silence.

Once they're safely inside their apartment, Tolya hangs up his coat and heads for his room without looking back. He gets it—boy, does he get it. This is a shitty limbo they're stuck in, and it's worse for Misha, because there's nothing he can do except wait. But he needs a minute, needs to breathe for a second and find a way to set his feelings aside before he can help Misha deal with his..

It's probably more like ten minutes once he comes out

of the bathroom and starts sorting through his suitcase, tossing dirty clothes in the hamper or the dry cleaning bag, taking his shaving kit back to its home in the cabinet under the bathroom sink.

He feels marginally better with everything in its place, order restored to his small corner of the world. Anyway, his stomach is reminding him that it's been hours since breakfast.

The apartment feels vacant when he ventures out of his room, none of the anger or drama he was expecting. Just absence. He checks Misha's room, just in case he's being paranoid, but both the bedroom and bathroom doors are standing open, the rooms obviously empty, Misha's suitcase standing abandoned next to the bed.

Checking the coat closet feels stupid, but it's not until he sees Misha's winter coat missing from its hanger that he starts to really worry, the vague unformed panic in his gut solidifying into something real.

He forces himself to stand, to breathe, to think. He needed space, quiet, time to process, and that's okay. Maybe Misha did, too. Maybe he just went for a walk. Maybe Tolya is taking after his babushka and worrying about nothing.

Pulling out his phone, he taps out a quick text. *u ok?*

The wait for a response seems interminable, but the phone screen doesn't even have time to go dark before it pops up. *ya, it's chill. just thinking, u know?*

Tolya lets out a breath he didn't know he was holding. *yeah. want 2 b alone?*

The shrug emoji is Misha's only response.

Throwing on his coat before he can think better of it, Tolya opens the door. He's got a pretty good idea where he's going.

Night before first preseason game

"What are you doing here?" Tolya asks, crossing the grass to the small swing set.

"Huh?" Mikey blinks at him. "Just, you know, thinking."

Tolya sits down in the empty swing. "You know, I've heard you can think anywhere. Even, and this may sound strange, but hear me out, in an apartment you're paying thousands of dollars a month for."

"Shut up," Mikey says, tipping his head back to look up at the sky.

When Tolya follows suit, all he can see is the light pollution from the downtown buildings, a haze of white and colors against the dark navy of the sky.

"I just needed some air," Mikey finally says. "We never had a very big house, and I had my own room, but I could always hear people. Sometimes I'd walk down to the park and sit on the swings, just to be somewhere quiet. I didn't even know this was here, can you believe it? I was just going for a walk, and here it is. Cool, huh?"

"Yeah," Tolya agrees. It is pretty nice. Cool enough to be pleasant after summer heat, but mild enough that a light

jacket is all they need to be comfortable. "Do you want to be alone?"

Mikey considers it for a moment, then shakes his head with a little smile. "Nah. I've gotten pretty used to having you around."

"Wow, thanks."

Rolling his eyes, Mikey shifts his weight until they bump together, sending Tolya swaying to the other side. "You know what I mean," he says, grinning.

"Yeah," Tolya agrees, dragging his feet over the ground until the swing comes back to equilibrium. "I know what you mean."

He has no idea how long they sit there that night, only that they do it together.

18

MIKEY

Mikey takes a shaky breath when Tolya's door closes behind him, holding it until he can feel the burning in his chest before letting it go. Standing here by the door just makes him feel like a dumbass, but the apartment seems too small all of a sudden, like the walls are closing in. Everything here is a reminder of Tolya, of him-and-Tolya and the unexpected unit they've become over the last few weeks. Of what he has to lose.

He forces himself to at least take his suitcase to his room, but then he's out the door again as fast as he can, hitting the elevator button too hard before changing his mind and heading for the staircase. Sure, they're on the tenth floor, but that's down, not up. Anyway, he hasn't worked out today, so this totally counts.

It's gonna be fine.

By the third flight down, he has regrets, his quads and knees aching, but he can't bring himself to come in from the stairwell and wait for the elevator, not where he might have to make small talk with people. Might have to pretend to be functional, when everything is collapsing around him.

He slows down, but keeps moving, one step at a time. The rhythm of it helps; the repetition. One-two-three-four-five-six-seven steps, then turn around the landing, the fingers of his casted hand brushing the cold metal of the railing. One-two-three-four-five-six-seven-turn, over and over, until the door out on ground level is almost a surprise.

Stepping out into the lobby, he crosses it with a purposeful step, nodding to the concierge at the desk. Nothing to see here, just someone on his way to a very definite destination, with no time to talk. He makes it to the other exit door without having to speak to anyone, pushes it open and steps out into the winter air.

Even though it's still a school break, it's cold enough even during the day that there are no children on the little playground. Mikey shoves his casted hand into his pocket, tucks his chin deeper into his hood as he makes his way toward the swing set and settles into the swing on the right.

Now that he's here, he has no idea what he was thinking. There are no answers here, no more than there were the other night when he and Tolya had come here. No sign, no god to pray to for a reprieve, no labors to accomplish. Nothing to do but what he does everywhere else.

Wait.

He can't even figure out why he's panicking about this so much. Yeah, Tolya's great; they click, and Mikey's been playing better with him than he ever has before. But this is the game; the buy-in is your life. You go where they send you, play for the team that pays you. He's known that almost as long as he's known hockey is what he wants.

But the thought of getting traded, of not seeing Tolya every day, of being hundreds or thousands of kilometers from Tolya—thinking about that leaves him breathless, like all the air got sucked out of the world.

And it's not even playing he's thinking about. Like, if he imagines never being able to play again—he forcefully shoves back the panic that rises with that thought, makes himself consider it, try to picture it.

Sure, life without hockey would suck. But he can imagine it, can see making a different life. Using his degree, probably, getting an internship and a job somewhere, wearing a suit and tie every day for something other than the pre-game time. But when he pictures it, he sees himself coming home at the end of the day to Tolya's smile, waking up in the morning to Tolya's sleep-rumpled face, meeting Tolya for lunch at one of their favorite places.

As if all this thinking has summoned him, Tolya pushes open the building door and walks outside, crunching across the dead grass to sit in the swing next to Mikey. Like everything's normal, like the world is still spinning along, like Mikey isn't trying to wrap his head around the fact that apparently he went and fell in love with his best friend without realizing.

"You okay?" Tolya asks quietly after a few minutes of silence.

"I—" Mikey abruptly realizes that Tolya has no idea what he's thinking. All he knows is that Mikey pitched a fit over his suitcase and then stormed out like a teenager throwing a tantrum. "Yeah, I think so. Sorry about before. I--you were just trying to help. I shouldn't have snapped at you."

Tolya shrugs, like it's no big deal, which somehow makes Mikey mad.

"No, really, Tolya. You don't deserve me putting my shit on you."

"Okay," Tolya says slowly. "But I can forgive you when you mess up, yeah?"

Mikey blinks rapidly, trying to chase away the prickling at the back of his eyelids. "Yeah, you can."

Tolya bumps their shoulders together, setting Mikey's swing swaying gently. "I do, you know. Forgive you. It's rough, right now. But it's gonna get better."

"Yeah, I just—" Mikey swallows around the lump rising in his throat. "I don't think I realized before today, why I'm really freaking out about this."

Silence hangs heavy between the, an almost physical

weight pressing down on them. Finally, just as he's about to break, Tolya speaks. "Yeah?"

Mikey almost, almost panics, makes up some bullshit about fucking up his CHL debut, about his career. But then he meets Tolya's eyes and the truth comes spilling out.

"I don't want to leave you."

Tolya blinks at him, something passing swiftly across his face before he arranges it in an encouraging smile. "I know. I don't want you to leave, either. But we'll still be friends, no matter where you are."

"No," Mikey says, trying to keep his tone even. "I mean, yeah, of course we will, but that's not why I don't want to leave you. I—I love you. Not like, I love you, bro, like I want to wake up with you every morning and hold your hand and maybe adopt a dog and a ton of kids someday love."

"I—really?"

Mikey does his best to parse the expressions moving across Tolya's face and fails. It's out there now, though, so he goes with it. "Really. But like, I get if that's not something you want. I just—" he shrugs. "You're my best friend. No matter who I'm in love with, you're the first person I want to tell. I know maybe this makes it weird—"

"Shut up," Tolya says, grabbing the chains of Mikey's swing and turning them to face each other. "I've been in love with you for—God, I don't even know how long. I didn't think you—"

It's Mikey's turn to interrupt, leaning in to kiss him.

This kiss is different, somehow, from the ones that came before. Not a "let's do it" kiss or a "that was so good kiss" or a "hello" or "good morning" kiss. There's something tentative about it at first, like it's their first kiss, even though they've kissed so many times, soft and sweet and new.

"I should've known," Mikey says when they break apart. "I should've known the first time we kissed.

Tolya shrugs, wrapping an arm around his waist to hold him closer and kissing him again. "I mean, nobody's ever accused you of being quick on the uptake."

"Hey!" Mikey smacks him on the shoulder with his casted hand, for the extra thump. "Isn't there something in the boyfriend rules about talking shit?"

A wondering look crosses Tolya's face, soft and open in a way that makes Mikey feel warm all over. "Is that what we are?"

"Boyfriends?" Mikey shrugs. "I mean, we're friends, we're boys, we're definitely together. So, yeah? If you want?"

That earns him a blinding smile and Tolya leaning in for another kiss. This one is hotter, hungrier, and Mikey finds himself falling into the familiarity of it.

"It's fucking freezing out here," Tolya mumbles, nuzzling his face into Mikey's neck. "Can we go upstairs and have boyfriend sex?"

"You have the best ideas," Mikey says, tilting his head to allow Tolya better access.

It takes a few minutes before they manage to disentangle themselves and head inside. Even then, Tolya keeps his arm around Mikey's waist, holding him close.

Making out on the elevator ride to their apartment is definitely the best part of being boyfriends

Second week of training camp

"Hey, you have a minute?" Tolly asks.

"Yeah, dude," Mikey says, pausing in front of his hotel room. "You wanna come in? Or we can go downstairs, get a beer."

Tolly hesitates for a moment. "Here's fine," he finally says. "If I have a drink, I might just pass out. Today was rough."

"For real." Mikey inserts his card in the lock and turns the handle. "Come on in. Sorry it's a mess."

"It's not that bad," Tolly says, even though his face tells another story as he steps over the random clothes lying around on the floor.

Mikey makes an attempt to gather them at least into a pile, pretty sure his mom is twitching randomly somewhere in Calgary at this very moment. "No, really, sorry. I've just been really tired, you know?"

"Yeah, for sure." Tolly sits down on the end of the bed, which is at least made, since the housekeeping service came through today. "So I wanted to ask, do you have any plans for a place to live after camp?"

"Shit, do I need plans?" Mikey asks, his mind whirling. Two minutes ago his biggest worry had been whether or not he had enough clean clothes to get through camp without using the hotel laundry. "You think I need plans?"

Tolly nods. "I mean, it's not sure until they tell you, but I played with some of these guys last year. They seem pretty confident that we're staying up. So I was thinking, if you want, we could get a place together. Since we're probably going to be on the same line."

"That sounds cool," Mikey says, before all his doubts can catch up. "I mean, are you sure you want to do that? I'm kind of a mess."

To do him credit, Tolly takes a minute to think about it. "I think so. I mean, it might not work out, but we're playing really well together. Like, I play better with you than I ever had before. So I'm in. If you are."

"Hell yeah," Mikey says. "So, like, how do we do this?"

"The front office has a list of realtors," Tolly says. "I can get it tomorrow and we can call somebody and start looking. Any dealbreakers for you?"

Mikey laughs. "I guess I don't have to worry about bugs and stuff, huh? I don't know, probably a decent sized kitchen. I warn you, if we get a place somewhere, my mom is gonna descend on us at least once. That's not so bad, she's a great cook, but she'll bring my sisters."

"That's fine," Tolly says. "I always wanted sisters."

"Take mine," Mikey says. "Please."

It's Tolly's turn to laugh. "Well, I'm sure I'll get to meet *them. Maybe we can sit down with the list of realtors tomorrow night and make a list of what we want?"*

"Sounds good." Mikey says. "You really know what you're doing with this adulting shit, don't you?"

"Not really," Tolly admits. "But I bet we can figure it out together."

19

TOLYA

"Stop," Tolya says when he catches Misha checking his phone for the fifteenth time in five minutes. Okay, that's probably an exaggeration. But not by much.

"Sorry." Misha looks a little shamefaced, tucking the phone into his pocket and turning his attention back to the TV screen.

Of course, it's only a minute or so later that his hand starts creeping back toward the phone again. Tolya reacts without thinking, grabbing his wrist and pulling it across his body.

Misha gasps, his eyes going wide

"Shit, did I hurt you?" he asks, starting to loosen his grasp.

"No, no," Misha says hastily. "It's fine. I—"

Tolya waits for several long heartbeats, but nothing else seems to be forthcoming. From the flush that's spread over Misha's cheeks and down his neck, it looks like maybe this is something sexual, something he's hesitant to talk about.

That's okay. Tolya can work with that.

Moving slowly this time, he reaches for Misha's other wrist with his free hand, wrapping his fingers carefully around it. "You want to tell me what you're thinking about?" he asks, squeezing gently.

Misha bites his lip, his pulse pounding against Tolya's fingertips. "I don't know, I—"

He falls silent without finishing the sentence.

"You like this?" Tolya asks, squeezing again.

"Yeah," Misha breathes.

Tolya leans in for a kiss, still holding on with both hands while he nibbles at Misha's lips, licks his way inside. It still blows his mind, that he gets to do this whenever he wants. That they're together, not just fucking around. He resolutely pushes any thoughts of what might happen today to the back of his mind. They could both use a little distraction right now, honestly.

"Okay," he says, lifting his head just enough to speak. "Can you tell me if I do something you don't like?"

Misha nods, straining toward Tolya like he wants nothing more in the world than to kiss him right now. Tolya meets him halfway, deepening the kiss hungrily.

He kind of misses Misha's hands on him, but this is good in a different way. Feeling Misha's muscles stretch and strain against his hands, he suddenly understands, deep in his gut and his bones, why people are into this.

When they break apart, both breathing like they've just come off a five-minute shift, Tolya has a plan, or at least half of one. "C'mon," he says, getting to his feet without letting go of Misha's wrists. "Bedroom."

It's a little complicated, making it down the hall without letting go, but Misha whimpers a protest when he starts to loosen his grip. Tolya finally compromises by getting one hand around both of his wrists, his fingers barely able to span them, and leading Misha down the hall to his bedroom. Misha's is closer, but Tolya can't help thinking, selfishly, that in case—in case something, he wants this memory.

"Take off your clothes for me," he orders, squeezing Misha's wrists one last time before letting go.

Apparently the command is enough to make up for not holding on any longer, because Misha quickly complies. Tolya gets a little lost in watching him, the way his muscles flex as he strips out of his t-shirt, the curve of his ass as he bends over to push his sweatpants down. He doesn't realize he forgot to take his own clothes off until Misha is standing there, completely naked, hard cock curving slightly up toward his stomach, looking at him expectantly.

"Lie down on the bed," Tolya orders. "On your back."

"Yes, sir," Misha murmurs, moving quickly to obey.

The bolt of electricity that sizzles down Tolya's spine at the words is unexpected, but he pushes that aside. This isn't about him. This is about Misha. Misha needs to be distracted, to forget, for a minute, what today is.

"Grab your legs and pull them back," he says, getting the lube from the bedside table, since it never quite seems to get put away.

The flush spreads further down Misha's chest as he complies, hooking his hands behind his knee and pulling them back toward his chest, spreading himself open. He makes such a pretty picture like this, his eyes wide and trusting.

"Think you can stay like that for awhile?" Tolya asks.

Misha opens his mouth, then hesitates, visibly thinking it over. "I don't know," he admits. "My right arm…"

Tolya nods. Despite pushing as hard as his physio will let him, his right arm still isn't a hundred percent. "It's okay," he soothes, running a hand down Misha's thigh because he can. He gets to. "I'll help you. Stay like this for me, okay?"

"Yeah. Yes." Misha's face settles into determined lines, his fingers tightening on his legs.

"Good."

Watching his flush deepen, the shiver that runs through his body at the word, is mesmerizing. Reluctantly, Tolya heads for the closet, looking back over his shoulder one last time before walking through the door.

Thankfully it only takes him a couple of minutes to find what he's looking for, the cheap ties his parents bought him back in juniors when he couldn't be bothered with anything other than a sloppy half-Windsor. He keeps meaning to donate them, but they're perfect for what he has in mind. Maybe he'll hold onto them awhile longer.

Misha just looks confused when Tolya walks back into the bedroom, holding the ties. At least, he does until Tolya sits down on the bed next to him and loops one end around his left wrist, tying the knot snug but not so tight that the fabric digs into the skin.

"That feel okay?" he asks, running a finger between the tie and Misha's skin.

"Yeah," Misha breathes, shivering a little when Tolya's finger slides over the thin skin at the base of his palm. "What—"

His question cuts off when Tolya grabs the free end of the tie and wraps it around his left thigh, pulling Misha's wrist down to rest against the bulge of his quad, his fingers curled around behind his knee. This part is trickier, but Tolya figures it out after a few false starts.

"There," he says, sitting back when he finishes and watching Misha tug experimentally against the restraint. "Too tight?"

"No." Misha's response is barely audible, soft and breathy and almost entirely made of air. "I—it's good."

He holds out his right wrist, a wordless request Tolya is helpless to ignore. The process goes more quickly now that Tolya isn't figuring it out on the fly. Within a few minutes, Misha is bound, hand to thigh, his legs spread open, knees pulled back toward his chest.

Tolya wishes he dared take a picture. It would almost

be worth the risk of a hack, of having their personal business spread across the internet, to have a permanent record
of this, of the way Misha's body almost seems to melt into
the bed, the tension seeping out of his muscles.

"Tell me if you need out," Tolya says, pulling his shirt
up over his head and throwing it aside. "Okay? Or if you
don't like anything."

Misha nods, his eyes wide and dark as he watches
Tolya climb onto the bed, settling on his stomach between
his legs. "I need to hear you say it, babe."

"I'll tell you," Misha says. "If I don't—if I don't like
something. Or if I need out."

"Good," Tolya approves, pressing an open-mouthed
kiss to Misha's inner thigh. He can't resist using his teeth a
little, sucking a little, until Misha is squirming under him.

He pulls back for a moment to appreciate the mark he
left behind, then repeats the process on the other thigh,
higher and closer to the sensitive crease of Misha's groin.

"You're gonna get chirped for these," he says, lifting his
head just enough that his breath moves across the wetness
he left on Misha's skin, making him shiver more. "You
okay with that? Everybody in the locker room is gonna see
these marks I left. They're gonna know you're mine."

"Oh, fuck," Misha whimpers, his cock twitching in the
corner of Tolya's vision.

"You like that?" Tolya asks. He sits up long enough to
grab a pillow, lifting Misha's hips and pushing it underneath. "You like everyone knowing you're mine?"

Misha swallows convulsively, the sound loud in the quiet room. "Yeah, yes, Tolya, please—"

"Shhh," Tolya soothes, nudging Misha's thighs further apart, reaching down and spreading him wide. "I've got you."

He settles onto his stomach again, licking slowly across the furled muscle of Misha's hole. Above him, Misha moans, a wordless, hungry sound. Tolya grins to himself before setting to work in earnest.

It's been awhile since the last time he did this. He'd forgotten how nearly meditative it was, kind of like skating can be sometimes. Time doesn't exist when he's like this; his world narrows down to just this moment, this bed. The noises Misha makes with every lick and nip and sucking kiss, the smell of sex filling the air, the flex of Misha's hamstrings against his shoulders, the soap-and-sweat taste of his skin under Tolya's tongue, this is all that exists.

"Tolya, Tolya," Misha gasps after some timeless interval. "Tolya—I want—I—fuck--please—"

Tolya fucks his tongue inside, shifts enough to nudge a finger in along with it. The stretch is awkward on his shoulders, but it's worth it for the way Misha whimpers, his hips hitching up off the bed as he tries to get Tolya deeper.

When his jaw starts to ache, Tolya adds another finger and sits up a little to better appreciate the sight before him. Misha is flushed almost all over, his skin covered in a fine sheen of sweat that only highlights the flex and ripple of his muscles as he writhes against the sheets.

"Too much?" Tolya asks softly, curling his fingers until they brush against the spot he was searching for.

"Nnnnaaahhh," Misha moans, his body going taut. A glistening drop of pre-come falls from the head of his cock to join the small puddle already on his abs. "Only—fuck—too much if you—stop."

Tolya grabs the lube and slicks his fingers before fucking in with three this time, unable to tear his eyes away from the spot where his fingers disappear into Misha's body. "Do you want me to stop?"

"No!" Misha's eyes snap open, his hands pulling at his legs to try to spread them wider. "No—please, please—don't stop—"

"Shhh," Tolya soothes, running a hand up and down Misha's shin. "I won't, sweetheart. Not unless you ask."

Misha relaxes back down onto the pillow, rolling his hips to try and get Tolya's fingers in deeper. "Not gonna—ah—happen."

Silence falls for a few moments, broken only by Misha's gasps and moans, by the wet, filthy sounds as Tolya fucks his fingers in and out.

"You gonna fuck me?" Misha finally asks, his voice shaky with arousal.

"Actually, I had something else in mind," Tolya says, stroking the sensitive skin of Misha's inner thigh. "If you think you can be good for me?"

Misha blinks at him with wide, dark eyes, swallowing

hard. His cock twitches in Tolya's peripheral vision. "I—yeah. Yeah, I can—yeah."

"Good," Tolya says, watching in fascination as Misha's eyes flutter closed. "Have you ever come untouched?"

"Is that a thing people do?" Misha asks, eyes opening again. "Like, for real, not just in porn?"

Tolya smiles at him. "Let's find out."

"Oh, God," Misha moans.

If he goes straight for the prostate, Tolya's pretty sure this is going to be over quickly. But Misha is so responsive, so turned on, that he can't help wanting to linger over it, to draw out as many sensations as possible.

They've had so much sex, but in a way he feels like he's just now learning Misha's body, his reactions. He's beautiful like this, so completely focused on the physical sensations that there's no room for anything else.

"Please, Tolya," he finally begs, "I don't think I can—just—please—just touch me—"

"You can," Tolya says, finally turning his full attention to Misha's prostate. It only takes one—two—three thrusts, dragging his fingers across that sensitive spot, before Misha curls in on himself and comes, liquid shooting thick and wet across his chest and stomach.

Tolya had been so caught up in what they were doing, so focused on Misha's reactions, that the sudden awareness of his own erection comes as a shock. He's suddenly desperate to come, barely hanging onto control.

Barely pausing long enough to grab the lube, he reaches for his cock, letting out a noise that's half sigh, half moan when he finally gets his hand on it. It's enough to catch Misha's attention, to get his eyes open again.

"On me," he says, watching Toya avidly.

The words make no sense in Tolya's brain, all of his attention focused on getting himself there, on what he needs. "Huh?"

"Come. On. Me." Misha says, enunciating each word.

And that—one last stroke, twisting around the head just the way he likes, and Tolya is complying, coming all over Misha's abs, until he can't any longer, until there's nothing left.

He really, really wants to just collapse on top of Misha, but this was his idea, his responsibility. He needs to take care of Misha. Taking a few breaths, he straightens up from his slump and reaches for the tie around Misha's left leg with shaking hands.

After a few fumbles, he manages to loosen the knot enough to let Misha slip his wrist free. Good enough. Repeating the process on the other tie goes marginally faster, and then Misha can stretch his legs out, groaning slightly.

"You okay?" Tolya asks, concern burning briefly through the post-orgasm haze. "Your legs, your arm—"

"They're fine," Misha interrupts, smiling softly up at him. "Just feels good to stretch, you know?"

Tolya nods. "Yeah. I'll go get—something to clean up with—"

"No, stay," Misha says, grabbing his arm and looking

up at him with pleading eyes before he can do more than shift his weight. "I wanna nap."

"You're gonna complain for like, an hour if you have to clean off dried jizz in the shower," Tolya warns half-heartedly.

Misha rolls to his side, flailing around with the hand not holding onto Tolya, and comes up with a t-shirt and a triumphant noise.

"That's my shirt," Tolya complains.

"Oh, like you actually want to get up and get a towel."

Misha starts to scrub at his chest and stomach, but Tolya bats his hand away and takes over, wiping more carefully at their combined mess until he looks reasonably clean.

"Nap now," Misha says when the t-shirt has been returned to the floor.

Tolya allows himself to be arranged to Misha's satisfaction, their limbs tangled together and the duvet pulled up over them. Honestly, despite his completely reasonable objections, a nap sounds pretty good right now.

The last thing he remembers before drifting off is the tickle of Misha's hair against his nose, the soft snores that tell him Misha is already out.

Tolya is jolted awake when Misha bolts out of bed. "'Izzit?" he mumbles, rubbing at his eyes just in time to see Misha's naked ass vanish out the door.

"What time is it?" Misha calls, the slap of bare feet on the floor receding. "Where's my fucking phone?"

Those words are enough to burn through the last post-nap haze, adrenaline spiking through Tolya's system. He honestly has no memory of leaving the bed; just one minute he's in it, the next he's standing in the living room watching Misha dig in the couch cushions for his phone.

He finally finds it, straightening with a little grunt of effort—then stands there, looking at it like it's a snake that might bite him.

"Do you want me to look?" Tolya finally asks.

"No," Misha says, squaring his shoulders. "I can do it."

Tolya rounds the couch, takes his free hand. "I know you can. But if you want me to—"

Misha presses his thumb to the fingerprint sensor with a sudden, jerky movement. Tolya's eyes go to the little phone icon first—he lets out a little breath at the same time Misha does—then dart up to the time display.

1:37 pm.

"No call," Misha says, his voice small. "They'd call, right?"

"They would," Tolya confirms, taking the phone out of his hand and setting it down on the coffee table. "It's past the deadline, Misha."

Misha blinks up at him, goes unresistingly when Tolya pulls him into his arms. "They didn't call?"

"They didn't call. You're not traded. You're staying here, with me." Tolya squeezes as gently as he can, trying to convey the same message with his touch.

His breath oofs out when Misha grabs on, holding tight, tight, his face tucked against Tolya's neck, hot and wet with tears.

Tolya has no idea how long they stand like that, and he doesn't care.

Misha isn't going anywhere.

"OKAY, LISTEN UP," Coach says, her voice snapping out over the low babble of the locker room. "Lines for tonight."

Silence mostly settles, faces turning toward her around the room. Tolya hears Misha take a deep breath, reaches out to squeeze his knee. This is the second time they've dressed him for a game since his injury, but last time he never made it off the bench. It was still unbelievably great, just having him there, but Tolya can practically feel the eagerness and apprehension radiating off him.

"—and Nirang and Gunnarson on defense," Coach is saying when he tunes back in. "Fourth line—"

Misha goes incredibly still next to him.

"—Chaudhari, Richardson, and Osaka, Petrov and Michaelson on defense." She pauses to let the whooping and cheering die down. "Welcome back, Mikey."

"Good to be back," Misha says, ducking his head, his face flushing.

Coach wraps up her pre-game speech and leaves them

to finish gearing up. "Hey," Tolya says, bumping his shoulder into Misha's. "Ready to light it up?"

"Yeah," Misha says, setting his jaw and checking the tape on his stick. "Let's do it."

Tolya feels like he's going to burst with excitement and anticipation for the rest of the pre-game routine, but he thinks he keeps it under control pretty well. Misha doesn't seem to notice anything out of the ordinary, but he's practically bouncing off the walls with excitement just to be back. He makes sure to be just behind Misha heading down the tunnel, filing onto the bench next to him.

Misha's always loved the pre-game show, small or large, he doesn't care, so as soon as his ass hits the bench, his face is turning toward the Jumbotron screen. It's perfect. Tolya wishes he had his phone, but Sarah from PR is there, just out of Misha's field of vision, her phone aimed right at him.

"Abs fans, are you ready?" the announcer's voice booms out, the crowd roaring in response. "Tonight, we have a very special game. Tonight, we welcome back number 44, Kevin Michaelson!"

Tolya only thought the crowd roared before. The noise this time is deafening, a solid wall of sound. He can't stop watching Misha's face, the way his forehead furrows before he gets it, the way his jaw drops slightly open as the Jumbotron shows a short montage of his time with the Abs, goals and hits, finally fading out on a still of his jersey number before showing a live shot of his face.

It takes a second for him to realize, to find the camera

operator. He smiles and waves directly to the camera, then gets to his feet, turning in a circle to acknowledge every part of the arena.

The slightly fading sound of the crowd redoubles, not starting to die down until he sits back down and the captains skate out onto center ice for the puck drop.

Tolya leans in, turning his head to whisper in Misha's ear.

"Welcome back."

First day of training camp

Tolya feels a little high on it when they finally leave the ice, from playing the kind of hockey he's dreamed of all his life. Michaelson—Mikey can practically read his mind, it seems. And it definitely works both ways.

It's only the first day of camp, and he's still using the names on jerseys to keep people straight, aside from the few guys he played with last year who also got called up for the camp. He files off the ice with the rest of them, following Mikey down the tunnel to the locker room to strip out of their gear.

"Hey," he says when they're seated, watching Mikey pull off his helmet and shake out his hair like a Bond girl.

"Hi," Mikey says with a grin, his teeth white in his neatly trimmed beard.

There's no telling how long they might have sat there

staring awkwardly at each other if one of the first-line d-men —Sunshine, Tolya thinks he's heard the other veterans calling him—didn't stop in front of them, clapping them each on the shoulder. "Louis," he proclaims, "I think this is the beginning of a beautiful friendship."

ACKNOWLEDGMENTS

It seems like I always say this, but there are so many people to thank. Hopefully I remember all of them (and if I don't, I'm going to blame mom brain).

Liz and Foz, as always, kept me going with their reactions to even the roughest of first draft chapters. To Katie, TD, and Charlotte for helping me with Canadianisms when my American ass had no idea what I'd messed up.

The OMGCP Discord, as always, has been so incredibly encouraging and patiently waiting; thanks for getting excited over stickers with me, y'all. And when I was stuck on the middle of this, the hockey discord, especially Jamesiee, Ant, Triodia, and witch-marner really helped me narrow down the tropes and situations I wanted to include; y'all are the best even if you do keep spamming me with cute pictures of Tyler Seguin (please never stop).

I always owe a huge thank you to the self-publishing Discord for validating my whining, and especially to

Aenaria for helping me with hockeying, since I am ignorant in many ways. Y'all are the best and always make my days better.

My Patreon supporters are amazing and incredible, especially for pointing out the weak spots in my first draft and starting the wheels turning so I could make it better.

To Dana (knifeshoeoreofight on Tumblr), thank you for letting me take your ideas and run with them; none of this would have happened without you.

I really am always so overwhelmed by the response to *Soft Hands* and *Three-Man Advantage*. Having these characters and worlds that I created out in the world, and all the people who love them, means so much to me. You, the readers, are my ray of hope when things seem dark. Thank you.

As always, last but never least, to Alex and Brittany for supporting me and cheering me on. I know this isn't your thing, but you're always there for me. I love our crazy life and I love you.

ABOUT THE AUTHOR

Ariel Bishop is an American romance and erotica author who feels strongly that all love triangles are best resolved through healthy polyamory. She lives in the Ozarks with her partners, their children and two bunnies that rejoice in the names Reginald von Pancakes and Snickers.

More information about her books can be found at her website or by signing up for her mailing list, and you can chat with her directly in her Facebook Group. You can also find her on Tumblr, Twitter, and Facebook. For sneak previews of upcoming books in the Tripping series and other rewards, you can support her on Patreon.

Keep reading for a list of her other works and a sneak peek at book 4 in the Tripping series, *Two Minutes!*

ALSO BY ARIEL BISHOP

Tripping Series

Soft Hands

Three-Man Advantage

Holding

Two Minutes (Coming February 2019)

TWO MINUTES SNEAK PEEK

Enjoy this sneak peek at Two Minutes, coming in February 2019!

CHAPTER 1

Cisco should have seen it coming.

It's not like he doesn't know what West is like. Everyone knows what West is like. The guy took a five-game suspension when the Jackalopes went the playoffs last year for slashing, for fucks sake, and the Gargoyles' winger almost lost the arm.

Chad S. West is basically everything Cisco hates about the way some d-men play, like anyone not on their team is collateral damage. Which, even ignoring how often people get traded, is a dumb way to be. Just don't be a dick, man.

Still, he's somehow surprised when West makes eye contact and fucking winks at him before lunging directly at Cisco's stick and then falling to the ice like the huge diva he is.

The ref's whistle shouldn't startle him, but apparently this is his day to be slow on the uptake. At least someone saw what West did. Cisco slides to a stop and waits for it. He can't wait to blow a kiss as West goes to the box for embellishment.

"Cross-checking, number 40, two minutes," the ref says.

Wait, what?

Stewie isn't on the ice, of course, because why would anything go right tonight? But Suzie is already skating over to the ref, arguing quietly but firmly, so Cisco stands there, holding his stick, and breathes. Because the alternative is using it on West's asshole face, and that'll get him more than a two-minute minor.

Apparently the ref is a Jackalopes fan, or just an asshole, because he isn't having any of it. None of Suzie's arguments are making a dent, and finally he skates away, mouthing "sorry" at Cisco, his face like a thundercloud.

Cisco takes a deep breath, lets it out, and heads for the penalty box. This is fine. It's bullshit, and anyone with eyes is gonna be able to tell that it's bullshit. But it's fine. The Jackalopes' power play unit is shit, nowhere near the Abs' penalty kill. He'll do his time in the sin bin, get back on the ice, and it'll be fine.

Only a small fraction of his attention is on where he's going. Mostly he's watching the line changes happen, the teams facing off for the puck drop. He steps through the open door to the box without really looking at the man in the suit who's holding it, just collapses in an ungraceful heap on the bench and pulls his gloves and helmet off, shaking his hair back out of his eyes. It's getting long enough that he probably needs to cut it soon.

"You cut your hair," a familiar voice says from his right. "It looks good."

Turning toward the voice is a completely involuntary reflex. Cisco couldn't have stopped himself if his life depended on watching the ice. That voice reaches down into his nervous system, commandeers control, and he doesn't even think he minds.

He's half-expecting to see a stranger when he turns. Just like any of a thousand, a million times he heard an almost-familiar voice or caught a glimpse out of the corner of his eye, only to discover he was imagining things.

But no. There he is, familiar dark hair and eyes. He's watching Cisco like he's not sure what to expect, which is fair enough. But he's there. Really there. When Cisco reaches out with a shaking hand, his arm is solid, warm under the fabric of his suit.

"Leo," he breathes, his voice barely audible.

The familiar mouth curves up just a little at the corners, like it always did when Cisco said his name. "Cisco," he says, and oh, that hurts, the familiar sound of that voice shaping the syllables of his name. "It's been —awhile."

Around one am on draft day, Cisco gives up on sleep and reaches for his phone. He pulls it under the sheets and duvet, turning on his side and using his body to block the light before unlocking the screen. If his mom is able to sleep, he wants to let her.

When he opens his texting app, his conversation with Leo is the first thing that pops up, obviously. He's probably asleep, but Cisco still taps out a quick can't sleep u up? *before switching over to his latest mindless time-wasting game.*

He's not expecting a response, but it still stings a little when he doesn't get one. Like, he gets Leo not coming with him. It's harder for goalies, fewer spots at the pro level. If their positions were reversed, he doesn't know if he could come with Leo, smile and clap while his boyfriend got the thing that he wants most in life.

So he gets it, but that doesn't mean that he doesn't miss Leo, doesn't wish he were here now. If he was here, they might have been able to get their own room; even though his mom's kind of old-fashioned in some ways, she knows how serious Cisco is about Leo. She basically treats them like they're engaged already, even if Cisco hasn't quite worked up enough nerve to pop the question.

But Leo isn't here, and Cisco's mom is. So he forces his mind away from the thoughts of what they could be doing if Leo was here, because like hell is he jerking off with his mom right there in the other bed. Even if she's sound asleep.

He plays the stupid game until the letters are swimming in front of his eyes, until he can't think of even simple three-

letter words. He's not sure when exactly he falls asleep, just that at some point he wakes up with sunlight glowing around the edge of the hotel curtains, his phone lying a few inches away from his hand.

When he checks the screen, Leo still has't replied.

Cisco's phone buzzes in his pocket while they're eating an early dinner. His stomach is roiling, but his mom is right; it's going to be a long night. He needs to eat.

It's probably just his abuela or one of his cousins texting to wish him luck, he thinks, and almost doesn't pull the phone out to check. It makes him sick, when he thinks about in the future, thinking about how he almost ignored it. But sometimes he thinks it would have been easier, not to know until later.

But there's no changing it. He fishes his phone out with one hand, using the other to cut off a bite of the tenderest salmon he's ever tasted.

When he looks down at the lock screen, the fork and the salmon clatter onto the floor unheeded.

"What's wrong, Chico?" His mom looks up from her grilled shrimp, her eyes widening at whatever she sees on his face.

He shakes his head, unable to speak. His tongue feels clumsy in his mouth, like forming words is beyond him. Instead he just hands her the phone, unlocked to show the text *from Leo's sister Elaine, the three short sentences that turned his world upside down in seconds.*

Leo had a breakdown. In hospital under observation. Dad didn't want me to tell you

"Oh," his mom says, more of an exhalation than a word. When she looks back up at him, her expression has firmed into decision, even though he can still see his own stunned grief reflected her eyes. "Do you want to leave? We can get a flight—"

"No," Cisco says, even though every beat of his heart is telling him otherwise. "No, I—I want to, but—his dad won't let me see him. I'm not officially anything. And if I miss the draft, he'll kick my ass himself when he gets out. No."

She nods slowly, setting the phone down and taking his hands in hers. "Okay. Then eat. You'll need your strength. He'll need you to be strong."

Cisco nods, asks their waitress for a new fork with a smile that feels like it will break his face. Forks up another bite of salmon and forces himself to chew and swallow even though it feels like dust and ashes in his mouth.

He needs to be strong for both of them, now.

"—the Alberta Abominables are pleased to select, from the University of Minnesota, Francisco Reyes."

Cisco shoves his phone with its blank screen hastily back into his pocket and stands, making his way to the stage, his mom holding his hand the whole way. He shakes the manag-

er's hand, and Stewart, the captain's hand, and the coach's hand—he can't remember her name, but that's okay, he'll get it. He puts the snapback on his head, pulls the jersey over his head. Smiles when he's told, looks into the camera when he's told, goes where he's told.

Everything is a blur, underlaid with the sick drumbeat of worry and fear quickly souring into anger. None of this matters. Why can't any of these people see that? The only thing that matters to him is lying in a hospital bed back in Minneapolis, and Cisco is stuck here with this bullshit.

He manages, somehow, to make it through without saying something incredibly offensive to his new organization. Thank fuck for his mom, papering over the cracks in his silences with her usual charm. It seems to take forever, but objectively he knows it's less than an hour before they escape, before it won't be horribly rude to check his phone.

The screen is still blank.

Their apartment feels empty, aching with it, when Cisco comes through the door. Even if he hadn't been told, he thinks he would have known something was wrong, just from the way the air hits his skin.

He drops his bag on the floor, kicking the door closed behind him in the same motion. Pulling his phone out is reflexive, even if there's nothing there. Elaine hasn't sent any other updates, and no one else in their family would talk to him even if he had their numbers.

There's absolutely zero chance that Leo has his phone, but he sends a text anyway, adding it to the end of all the unanswered texts he's sent since draft day, just because he can't—he has to do something. *Anything. He's not giving up on them without a fight. Even if he doesn't know who to fight, how to fight, just yet.*

Miss you. Love you. Talk to me soon, please.

He doesn't leave the first voicemail until much later, much drunker.

"Leo? Baby, I know you can't get this now, I know you—just call me, please. I love you, I just—I just want to hear your voice. Please"

"Baby, it's been a month. Elaine won't talk to me, I don't know if your dad got to her, but—look, if you need time, if you need space—I'll give you whatever you need. Just—please —it doesn't have to be you. I don't—I need to know that you're alive. Please, baby."

"I have to go to training camp. I don't know what to do with your stuff. I boxed it up and left it with Lightning—Seth. I hope—I hope you're okay. That's all I want, you know."

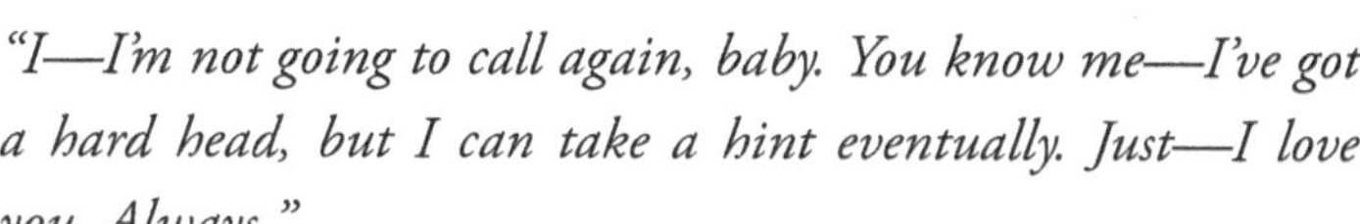

"I—I'm not going to call again, baby. You know me—I've got a hard head, but I can take a hint eventually. Just—I love you. Always."

Cisco knows he's staring, but he can't look away. Maybe he's hallucinating, maybe if he takes his eyes off Leo, he'll vanish again, gone for another seven years. Maybe this is just the ghost of Leo, of all the hope and love that he used to feel.

What does he say? What can he say, that he didn't say in the texts or the voicemails or the emails that he sent off into the void, unacknowledged and unreturned. Like the Flying Dutchman, ghost messages coursing through the darkness.

"Leo," he says again, his voice hoarse. "I—"

Before he can come up with any more words, the buzzer sounds.

"Your two minutes are up," Leo says, never looking away from him.

When Cisco tears his eyes away, he sees the PK unit heading back toward the bench. He sees Stewie waving him back out onto the ice.

Every beat of his heart says to stay here, not to let Leo slip through his fingers again. But—

"Your team needs you."

Cisco nods at Leo's words, buckles his helmet back on and shoves his hands into his gloves.

Stepping back out onto the ice isn't the hardest thing he's ever done, but it hurts, just the same.

When he glances back at the box, Leo is watching him go.

www.ingramcontent.com/pod-product-compliance
Lightning Source LLC
Chambersburg PA
CBHW050558190726
48283CB00007B/2195